Revenge, Rescue, and Revelations

Misadventure and Mystery, Volume 3

Travis Cramer

Published by Travis Cramer, 2024.

This is a work of fiction. Similarities to real people, places, or events are entirely coincidental.

REVENGE, RESCUE, AND REVELATIONS

First edition. July 31, 2024.

Copyright © 2024 Travis Cramer.

ISBN: 979-8227354501

Written by Travis Cramer.

Also by Travis Cramer

Misadventure and Mystery
Cars, Computers, and Chaos
Secrets, Suspicions, and Silence
Revenge, Rescue, and Revelations
Kidnappers, Killers, and Karma
Presents, Poison, and Peril
Hitmen, Hunches, and Havoc - Part 1
Hitmen, Hunches, and Havoc - Part 2

Watch for more at https://books2read.com/ap/81Do3O/
Travis-Cramer.

Table of Contents

Revenge, Rescue, and Revelations

By Travis Cramer

Edited by Violet Cramer

Chapter I

"Teddy, I'm going to kill you!" Erica had been helping Teddy practice his passing with a soccer ball when Teddy suddenly launched the ball straight into a wooden birdhouse that was hanging on a tree branch, shattering it into pieces and completely wrecking it.

Teddy put his hand over his mouth. "Oops," he said simply.

Erica shook her head and walked over to the birdhouse. "This was a birthday gift from Adrian," she said, kneeling down and picking up one of the pieces.

"Sorry," Teddy said meekly. "I didn't think I kicked the ball that hard. I'll help you fix it."

"No, you can't fix it," said Erica. "Just help me clean up the mess. Go get a garbage bag from inside."

"Alright," Teddy said, running inside.

"Siblings," Erica muttered to herself. She loved her younger siblings and all, but she couldn't deny that they could really be obnoxious sometimes.

"I feel your pain," a voice said from in front of Erica. Erica looked up and saw Adrian standing next to the broken birdhouse.

"Oh, Adrian, hi," Erica said, putting the piece down. "Sorry about the birdhouse. I know it was a present from you."

Adrian shrugged. "It's okay. I can just make you a new one. What happened?"

"Teddy kicked the soccer ball too hard and hit the birdhouse," Erica said, sighing. "I probably should have seen it coming, but I really didn't think that he could kick it that hard."

"That's exactly how I feel about Katie!" said Adrian. "Every time I think that there's no way she can do something wrong or mess something up, she does the unthinkable and I have to clean the mess up."

Erica stood up. "I'm a little jealous of Phoebe. Being an only child must be great."

"Erica, I got the bag!" Teddy called, running over to Erica.

"Great, you can start throwing the pieces away," Erica said, gesturing to the mess on the ground.

"Aren't you going to help?" Teddy complained.

"Hey, you broke it," said Erica. "You can clean it up."

"Fine," Teddy grumbled and started throwing the wood in the bag.

"What are you doing here?" Erica asked Adrian. "I assume you didn't get magically summoned here after Teddy broke the birdhouse."

Adrian laughed. "No, I wanted to ask you something. My parents are pressuring me to take up a sport."

"Okay..." Erica said, a little confused.

"Well, I figured that since you're the "sports queen", you would be the person to ask about picking a sport," Adrian said.

"Oh, I see," Erica said. "Well, I'm sure I can find a sport for you. What about soccer? I heard the boys' team needs a new defense."

'No, I was thinking about taking up something more like karate or ju-jitsu," Adrian said. "Something that can help me learn to fight."

Erica scratched her head. "I've never really pictured you as a fighter," she said. "Why do you want to learn all of a sudden?"

"I've just been thinking about everything that's been going on these past few weeks, and I'm realizing that I'm pretty useless in a fight," Adrian replied.

"That's okay," Erica said. "Fighting's probably not your thing. You're good at other things."

"Great, but I'll never know if fighting is my thing or not if I don't try and learn," Adrian answered. "I just wanted to know which sport you would recommend."

"None," Erica answered. "I don't suggest that you take up any fighting sports."

Adrian looked confused. "Why not?" he asked. "You don't think it's an important skill to have?"

"Not for you," Erica replied. "For some people, sure. But I just don't think that it would suit you. If you were to take lessons, you'd probably hate it, but you'd force yourself to take it anyway, because you hate quitting things."Adrian sighed. "You're probably right. But I want to be useful and not just the person who tags along."

"You are useful," said Erica. "Just because you can't fight doesn't make you useless. You're smart, and you can get out of tough situations. Plus, you have plenty of skills that none of us have."

"Phoebe is smart," Adrian said. "And what skills do I have?"

"Okay, first of all, Phoebe is book-smart," said Erica. "You're better at thinking outside the box. And if I recall correctly, you were the one who knew how to escape from ropes. Neither I, nor Scott, nor Phoebe know how to do that. So, forget about trying to learn how to fight and join the soccer or baseball team instead."

Adrian chuckled. "Alright, I'll try out for the baseball team. I used to be pretty good when I was younger anyway, so I guess it can't hurt."

"Baseball stinks," Teddy said, throwing the last piece of wood into the bag. "You should play hockey."

"I don't even know how to skate," said Adrian.

"Ignore him," said Erica. "He hates baseball because last time he played a game, he struck out every time."

"The umpire was cheating, okay," Teddy protested. "He called foul balls on me when they were clearly good."

Erica rolled her eyes. "Yeah, okay." She turned to Adrian. "Baseball tryouts start in a few days. You should check the practice schedule to make sure the practices don't conflict with anything else on your schedule."

"My schedule's pretty open right now except for driving lessons on Monday and Wednesday, but I'll check," Adrian said. "Thanks for the help!"

"Of course," said Erica. "I'll see you at school tomorrow."

Adrian nodded and left on his bike, leaving Erica with Teddy. Teddy handed the bag to Erica and said "All done. Can we go back to practicing again?"

Erica shook her head. "Are you kidding?" she asked.

Upset, Teddy tossed the bag onto the ground and went back inside. Sighing, Erica picked up the bag and took it over to the trash can next to the house. She was walking back towards the house when she noticed that there was a police car parked outside her house.

A little confused, Erica walked towards the police car, thinking it was Officer McKinley or Miles. Strangely, though, when she got close enough to the police car to see who was inside, the car drove off, leaving Erica puzzled.

Erica watched the police car drive off and shrugged. "Probably a speed trap or something," she thought to herself.

She went back inside and sat down in front of her computer, figuring it was probably time to start doing her homework.

THE NEXT DAY AT SCHOOL, the four friends met up at the lunch table at school like they always did.

"What did you think of our sub for Algebra 1 today?" Scott asked Erica with his mouth full.

Phoebe scowled. "What did I tell you about talking with your mouth full?" she asked.

"I wasn't talking to you!" Scott said, swallowing. "I was talking to Erica." He looked at Erica who was distractedly staring at the wall across from them.

"Hello, earth to Erica," Adrian said, rapping on the table.

Erica jumped. "Sorry, what were you saying?" she asked.

"You've been out of it all day," Scott said. "What's going on with you?"

"Nothing really," said Erica. "Just been thinking a lot lately."

"What about?" Adrian asked. "College?"

Erica made a face. "Not yet," she said. "I'd like to finish high school first. No, I've been thinking about all the sports I play. I'm starting to wonder if it's causing my grades to suffer."

"What do you mean?" asked Phoebe. "You're not failing high school or anything."

"Well, no, but I've noticed that my grades aren't as good as any of yours," Erica said. "I think I might not be spending enough time studying and too much time practicing sports."

"So, are you thinking of quitting sports?" Scott asked. "You love sports."

"Not entirely, but I might cut out some of them," Erica answered. "Maybe only play 1 or 2 sports instead of the 5 that I'm playing now."

"Do you really think it's affecting your grades that much?" Adrian asked.

"I don't know. It's the only thing that I can think of," Erica said. "Now that I'm a sophomore, classes are much harder, and I don't think I'm putting enough time into my homework."

"I wouldn't say 'much harder,'" Phoebe said.

"You don't count," Erica answered. "You're taking Calculus and I'm still struggling with Algebra 2."

"Maybe your mind is just occupied with other things," said Adrian. "Are you sure that you're not still being reminded about what happened to you before?"

A couple of weeks prior, Erica had been kidnapped by two ex-police officers and forced to help them rob houses. Eventually, Officer Miles had captured them with Scott, Adrian, Phoebe, and Erica's help, but it had still been a traumatizing experience for Erica.

Erica shrugged. "I've been trying to forget about it, but it keeps coming back."

"I don't think that sports are your problem," Scott said. "You need to put what happened to you in the past and focus on other things."

"I'm trying, okay," said Erica. "But it's not really something that I can just brush off and forget about."

"We aren't saying that," Phoebe broke in. "Just that constantly thinking about that is probably what's making your grades suffer. It might also be impacting your sports as well."

"So, what do you recommend I do?" Erica asked. "The band was supposed to help me forget about it, but I don't really think that it's doing the job. I still have nightmares."

Chapter II

"You need a vacation," said Adrian. "Actually, my parents were planning to take the RV out for a week-long trip family trip in a few days. I was actually going to tell you guys today, but I'm sure my parents wouldn't mind if I invited you along."

"I wouldn't want to impose..." Erica said. "I'd just get in the way. Besides, what about school?"

"My parents already cleared it with the principal and teachers. We won't be missing any important tests or quizzes, and I'm sure we can take our textbooks with us," Adrian said. "Trust me, you wouldn't be imposing. Besides, I need someone to come with me. Road trips with just Katie and my parents are really the worst sometimes."

"I don't know..." Erica didn't sound convinced. "Are you sure your parents wouldn't mind?"

"Positive," Adrian replied. "I can ask them after we get home from school today."

Erica scratched her head. "I've never been in an RV before. It sounds cramped and, no offense, but really uncomfortable."

"It's actually not," Scott broke in. "My parents rented an RV for camping trip a few months ago, and it was pretty luxurious. You should really go with Adrian."

"What about you and Phoebe?" Erica asked.

"What about us?" Phoebe asked. "We'll stay at home and nothing will be different for us."

"Won't you be missing out?" said Erica.

Phoebe snorted. "Vacations are not my cup of tea," she said. "I'd rather stay at home and spend my hours studying."

"And I have a bunch of things that I need to catch up on," Scott said. "Really Erica, you should go. It'll help clear your mind, and you might need a break from school and sports."

"Okay, okay, you've convinced me," Erica said. "I'll ask my parents if I can go after school."

"Awesome!" said Adrian. "And I promise that you'll love traveling in an RV. It's super fun."

The four of them finished up their lunch and headed back to class. When the bell rang, dismissing them, they all headed home. And a few hours later, Erica texted saying "My parents said I could go!"

Adrian texted back "That's great, because my parents said it was fine if you went along."

Erica texted "So, it's settled."

A few days later, Scott and Phoebe were helping Erica and Adrian pack their stuff into the RV after school.

"So, do you know where you guys are going?" Scott asked.

"Michigan," said Adrian. "It's a place that my parents and I have wanted to go to for a long time. My dad's a big fishing nut, and he wants to go fishing in the great lakes. I personally just like cool weather."

"We should have gone to Florida," Katie interrupted. "That's where I want to go."

"Katie just wants to go to Disney World," Adrian explained. "We've already been there once, but she wants to go again."

"What time are you leaving?" Phoebe asked. "Also, who's driving this giant thing."

Adrian looked at the RV. It was a large, 45 foot long, Class A RV. Definitely not something he would want to drive. "My dad is," he said. "He used to be a trucker, so he's used to driving giant vehicles like these. Also, we should be leaving in about an hour."

Erica tossed her last bag into a storage compartment on the side of the RV. "And you're sure this thing is safe?" she asked, looking at the length of the RV.

"Of course, it is," said Adrian. "We made sure to get everything checked out before we made this trip."

Erica shrugged. "All right, but if we crash, I'm blaming you."

Adrian and Scott laughed. "You'll be fine," Adrian said. He spotted his dad lugging a heavy duffel bag towards the RV and ran over to help him.

"So, how are you feeling about this?" Phoebe asked Erica.

"Well, it will be nice to get away from North Carolina for a while," Erica said. "Hopefully it'll help me forget about all the things that have happened."

Scott nodded. "That is the whole point of this vacation."

"And you're sure neither of you wanted to go?" Erica asked.

Scott and Phoebe both nodded. "Absolutely sure," Phoebe said. "We'll keep you updated with everything that's happening back at home."

"As long as you send us pictures of Michigan," Scott said, laughing.

Erica laughed. "Of course, I'll send you guys' pictures. What's a vacation without photos to help you remember all the disastrous things that happened?"

"And I'll make sure to send you a fish, Phoebe," Adrian said, heaving the heavy duffel bag into the RV.

Phoebe gagged. "You'd better not," she said. "There's nothing grosser then a slimy, raw, wet fish."

Adrian grinned. "I can think of at least a dozen things that are nastier."

Phoebe rolled her eyes as Adrian's dad tossed the last bag into the RV. "That's the last of them," he said. "Everyone do a clean sweep and make sure they got everything. Then we can be on our way."

He walked over to Erica and asked, "Are you sure you have everything you need?"

Erica nodded and said "I put my stuff in the overhead compartment in my bedroom."

"Perfect." Adrian's dad shut the RV door and headed back inside to double-check everything.

"Well, I guess we'll see you guys in a couple of weeks," Scott said. "Have fun on vacation!"

"And I'll make sure to keep you up-to-date on all our classes," Phoebe said, half-jokingly.

Adrian and Erica climbed into the RV just as Adrian's parents came outside. Katie was already inside the RV, rummaging through the fridge, seeing what they had brought with them.

Adrian's mom locked the door and both parents climbed into the RV. Adrian's dad took the driver's seat and said, "Everybody, buckle up. We've got a long drive ahead of us."

Erica buckled her seatbelt as the RV started and hung her sweatshirt on the hook behind the seat. Adrian leaned outside the window and called out to Scott. "Don't forget, my plants need to be watered twice. Once in the morning before school, and again after school."

Scott had volunteered to maintain Adrian's garden while they were on vacation, and Adrian was very particular about what Scott should and shouldn't do.

"And remember not to water them too much, or you'll kill them. And if any of them start to look droopy, give them a teaspoon of the fertilizer in the bag next to pots."

"I know, Adrian," Scott called back. "Don't worry about your garden, I'll take good care of it."

"Adrian, seatbelt," Adrian's dad interjected. Adrian buckled his seatbelt up, and made sure Katie was buckled in as well. Scott and Phoebe both waved goodbye to them as Adrian's dad pulled the RV out of the driveway and onto the road.

Scott and Phoebe watched as Adrian's dad drove the RV down the road. They stood there watching until the RV was out of sight and Scott said, "I hope this helps get Erica's mind off everything."

"Nothing like a week-long vacation to clear your head," Phoebe responded. "At least for some people, anyway."

"Do you really not like vacations?" Scott asked. "I don't know any person who doesn't enjoy spending some time away from home and school."

"Sure, you do," Phoebe said. "Me! I just don't like vacations, since I think they're a complete waste of time."

"It's fun to waste time sometimes, though," Scott responded. "All work and no play makes Jack a dull boy."

"Your name is Scott, not Jack. And it should be 'make' not 'makes,'" said Phoebe.

"No, it's just a saying-whatever," Scott said, giving up. "What *do* you like to do for fun?"

"Read," said Phoebe. "And write."

"No, for fun," said Scott. "Not for school."

"School *is* fun," Phoebe answered. "Unlike some people, I find filling my brain with knowledge enjoyable. Much more enjoyable than emptying my brain of everything."

Scott shook his head and grabbed his bike that was leaning against a telephone pole. "I give up. You really are a strange person."

"I am not," Phoebe protested. "I just like learning."

"That's strange," Scott said, pedaling away. "Just ask anyone at school."

Scowling, Phoebe hopped on her bike and chased after Scott. He had a head start, though, and he was taller than her, so Phoebe eventually got left in the dust.

ABOUT 3 HOURS INTO the trip, Erica asked Adrian, "Am I allowed to stand up and walk around?"

Adrian, who was looking at his phone, shrugged. "Technically, no, but if we're on a flat, straight road, it's fine."

Erica peered out the windshield and said, "Looks pretty flat to me." She unbuckled her seat belt and stood up from her seat. Adrian followed suit and asked Erica, "So, what do you think of riding in an RV?"

"It's weird," said Erica. "It's basically a hotel, but on wheels. I also never get my own bedroom when we go on vacation."

"Well, it's not really a bedroom, per say," said Adrian. "It's just a section of the RV that's closed off."

"Works for me," said Erica. She peered out the window and asked "How long is the drive to Michigan?"

"Dad said it's a 14-hour drive, but we're stopping over in a campground in Ohio," Adrian replied. "He didn't want to drive the full 14-hour drive in 1 day."

"Makes sense, I guess," Erica said. She walked over to her bedroom and climbed onto the bed. "Oof," she said. The mattress wasn't the most comfortable thing in the world.

"There's a futon in the closet," Adrian called from the cab. "The mattresses in this aren't very soft, so we usually put those on top of the mattress to make it more comfortable."

Erica dug the futon out of the closet and plopped it on top of the mattress. She hopped on the bed again and shrugged. It was slightly better, but still didn't feel that great.

"Erica, we're getting off the highway soon, so you should sit down," Adrian's father called from up front. "The road's going to get bumpier."

Erica took a seat next to Adrian and said, "This feels strange. I've never been on a vacation without the rest of my family."

"I don't think the RV would have fit all of us," said Adrian. "There's only 4 'bedrooms', plus a couch and table that convert to a bed."

"They didn't want to come, anyway," said Erica. "I wonder what Scott and Phoebe are doing."

LIKE MOST SUNDAY AFTERNOONS, Phoebe was lying on her bed, getting lost in a book. It was only 10am, so there was still plenty of time for her to get through the entirety of "The Red Badge of Courage."

At least, there was, until the doorbell rang. Since her parents had gone out shopping, leaving Phoebe home alone, she sighed and reluctantly closed her book. She climbed off her bed and headed downstairs to see who could be at the door this early in the morning.

She was surprised to see Scott standing there, but she was even more surprised when she was Officer McKinley and Officer Miles standing behind him.

"What's going on?" Phoebe asked, puzzled. McKinley stepped forward and said "We have some distressing news."

Now a little concerned, Phoebe asked, "What do you mean 'distressing'?"

This time, it was Officer Miles that answered. And she didn't mince words. "The two thieves that kidnapped you four has escaped," she said bluntly.

Phoebe stepped back. "They did what?" she asked, hoping she heard wrong.

"Escaped," Scott broke in. "Officer McKinley told me already."

"How did this happen?" Phoebe asked, not sure if she was nervous or angry. She couldn't tell what she was feeling.

"They were being transferred from the (add town name) Prison to the North Carolina State Prison, when the brakes on the truck suddenly gave out," Miles said. "The driver crashed into a building, giving the prisoners the perfect opportunity to escape."

"How did the brakes on the truck go out?" Phoebe asked.

"Someone tampered with them before the prisoners were transported. The brake line was sliced, and it snapped during the drive to the prison," McKinley said. "The kidnappers must have planned the escape in advance."

"So, what do we do?" asked Phoebe. "Are they going to come after us?"

"That's what we're concerned about," Miles answered. "But I think that Erica is in the most danger."

"Erica's on vacation with Adrian and his family," said Scott. "You don't think that they're going to come after them, do you?"

"We're not sure yet," said McKinley. "We don't even know if they are going to come after any of you. They might take this opportunity to flee the country."

"They're not going to," said Phoebe. McKinley, Scott, and Miles all looked at her, confused. "How do you know that?" Miles asked.

"It's logic," Phoebe responded. "Once they knew that Erica had told the police about them, they didn't flee. They came right after Erica. It only stands to reason that they're going to come after her again."

"She's right," Scott said, thinking about it. "But Erica's on vacation with Adrian. There's no way the thieves could know where's she going, right?"

"We hope not," said McKinley. "But they escaped hours ago, and we don't know where they are or what they know."

"That's an eerie thought," Phoebe said. "What should we do?"

"You two? Nothing," Miles said. "There's no reason to put yourselves in more danger than necessary. Meanwhile, the entire police department will do everything they can in order to catch them."

"What if they come after us?" Phoebe asked. "We got kidnapped along with Erica when we attempted to rescue her."

"It's unlikely that they will," said McKinley. "And they don't have your address, so they don't know where to find you."

"That's true," said Scott. "They only tracked Erica's phone, not ours. They might not have even known we existed if we hadn't seen them drive away from the police station."

"Exactly," said Miles. "They do know about your store, so I advised your parents to up their security system and we assigned two officers to patrol the area when the store is opened."

"Should we tell Erica about this?" Scott asked. "I feel like she should know."

"That's up to you," said Miles. "The odds that the thieves will track Erica down across the country are slim, but if you feel like she should know, feel free to tell her."

"I don't think we should," Phoebe said. "She went on this vacation on Adrian to forget about everything and if well tell her that the thieves just escaped, that will just remind her about everything that happened."

Scott nodded. "You're right. For now, it's probably better that she doesn't know."

"Like I said, it's up to you," said Miles. "But if we find evidence that indicates that the thieves are going after Erica, we'll warn her first thing."

"For now, though, you two just need to be careful and watch your back," McKinley said. "I'd avoid going places by yourself, just to be on the safe side."

"You said that it was unlikely that they would come after us," said Scott.

"It is, but there's no guarantee," Miles answered. "After all, we thought they would leave town after Erica told us about them, but they went after her instead, so it's always a good idea to take precautions."

Miles' walkie-talkie went off and she turned to McKinley. "We have to get back to the station," she said. Turning back to Phoebe and Scott, she said, "Be careful. If you see something suspicious, don't hesitate to give me a call."

Phoebe and Scott both nodded and the two officers walked back to the cruiser and drove off. Scott and Phoebe watched as they drove off, both of them hoping that the thieves wouldn't come after them.

Phoebe gestured to her front door. "Do you want to come inside?" she asked Scott. "McKinley said that we shouldn't go places by ourselves."

Scott half-laughed. "Sure, I'll come inside," he said. "As long as I'm not interrupting anything."

"No, I was just reading," Phoebe said, walking into the house. Scott followed her and said, "Now I'm thinking that we should have gone with Erica and Adrian to Michigan."

"Shhh," said Phoebe. "Don't tell anybody where they were going. That just tells the thieves exactly where to go."

"We're inside your house, Phoebe," Scott said. "Who's going to be listening to us here?"

Phoebe shrugged. "I don't know, but it's best not to take chances."

"I guess so," Scott said, not fully convinced. "Hopefully Erica and Adrian are at least enjoying their vacation."

Chapter III

"Woah, geez!" Erica said, almost sliding off her seat again. "What road are we driving on? The Appalachian Trail?"

"It's a winding road," Adrian's dad said. "It's hard to keep something as big as this on the road without jolting it a bit."

"I've noticed-oof!" Erica's arm slammed into the wall next to her. "Please tell me we're getting back on the highway soon."

Adrian glanced over at his dad's phone screen. "According to the directions, we'll-yikes." Adrian was pushed to the side as his dad made a sudden turn. "We'll get back on the highway in about 10 minutes."

"Is the road going to stay this winding for the whole 10 minutes?" Erica groaned, rubbing her arm. "Where's Katie?" she asked, glancing over at Katie's empty seat.

"In her bedroom," Adrian said. "Apparently this road doesn't bother her much."

"Lucky her," said Erica. She looked around the RV and asked, "Is there any chance that I could get something to eat?"

"I wouldn't recommend it," Adrian answered, grabbing the side of the table to prevent himself from pulling on his seatbelt. "The minute you open that fridge, everything's going to fall out."

Erica sighed. "How long until we get to the campsite?" she asked.

"Uhh, 5 hours and 32 minutes," Adrian said, glancing at his father's phone again. "But once we get back on the highway we can get up and walk around."

"Awesome," Erica said, leaning back in her chair. "How often do you guys take this RV out, anyway?"

"Well, usually 2-3 times a year," said Adrian. "This is the second time this year."

"And Adrian's going to drive it once he gets his license," Katie called, sticking her head out from her room.

Adrian winced. "Stop saying that, Katie!" he called back.

"What, you don't want to drive this?" Erica asked. "Why not?"

"Was that a rhetoric question, or are you actually-" Adrian was cut off by a loud bang and suddenly the RV started shaking wildly.

"What happened?" Erica, Adrian and Katie asked at the same time, as they were being bounced around.

Adrian's dad hit the brakes and skidded to a stop on the side of the road. "I'd say we got a flat tire," he said, getting up from his chair. He opened the RV door and everyone stepped outside.

Adrian walked over to the back of the RV and looked at the tires. "These look fine to me," he said, giving both of them a good kick.

"Not these," Erica called from the other side of the RV. The rest of them joined her at the tire and Adrian's dad shook his head. The tire was completely blown. "I don't understand," he said. "We just got the RV inspected a few days ago and they said the tires were fine."

"You must have hit something," Adrian's mom broke in. "Although on a road like this, I don't know what there is to hit."

Adrian's dad sighed. "Well, we might as well get the spare tire on," he said. "Adrian, Erica, can you two get the jack out while I start up the generator?"

The RV came with an electric jack, but naturally, it needed to be plugged in to be used. Thankfully, the RV had a generator which provided power to the whole vehicle.

"Sure," Adrian said, walking over to the back of the RV where the jack was stored. Erica followed him and asked, "Has this ever happened before?"

Adrian shook his head. "Nope, first time we've gotten a flat on our RV." He pried a panel off the back of the RV, revealing the jack. "Here, this thing is heavy. Can you give me a hand?"

"Of course," Erica answered, leaning in to help him. Together they were able to pull out the jack and lug it over to the tire. Breathing heavily, Adrian said to Erica, "There's a lug wrench set in the compartment. Can you grab them?"

Erica nodded and went back to the compartment. Adrian's dad started the generator up and Adrian plugged the jack in. Adrian's dad positioned it under the RV frame and when Erica returned with the wrenches, Adrian turned the jack on and waited for it to raise the RV.

There was a grinding sound, and suddenly all the lights in the RV flickered. Except the jack didn't go up. Confused, Adrian turned it off again and asked his dad, "Did I do it wrong or something?"

Adrian's dad flipped through the manual that came with the jack. "Don't think so," he said. "Try it again."

Adrian obliged and hit the switch again. This time, instead of a grinding noise, they all saw a large spark fly from the motor followed by a loud pop, which made them all jump. Then the jack turned off entirely.

"Well, that's not good," Adrian's dad said. He hit the switch again, but this time there was no response at all.

"Fantastic," said Adrian. "We're stranded in the middle of nowhere with a flat tire and no way to change it out."

"And we have no cell signal," Erica said, holding her phone up.

"Seriously?" Adrian asked. "This is straight out of a corny adventure novel. Does the RV have a hand crank jack?"

Adrian's dad shook his head. "No, just the electric jack." He knelt down and inspected the jack. The motor smelled burnt and there was still smoke coming out.

"I wouldn't get to close to that," Adrian said. "It looks like it's about ready to explode."

"Yeah..." Adrian's dad unplugged the jack and pulled it away from the RV. "Well, without cell signal and no way to change the tire, I guess we just have to wait until another car comes by."

"We've been here about 20 minutes already, and I haven't seen another car drive down this road," Erica said. "We might be here for a while."

"Well, I guess it's a good thing that we're basically in a house on wheels," Adrian said, climbing back into the RV." He came back out shortly holding a stack of fluorescent orange triangles. He placed a 2 in front of the RV, 2 in the back, and 2 on each side.

"That should alert anyone passing by that we need help," Adrian said, climbing back into the RV. "We might as well get something to eat while we're waiting."

The rest of them followed Adrian back into the RV and they all took a seat on one of the RV's chairs. Adrian's Mom pulled out a Tupperware container and started heating up the contents.

"Well, this is not how I imagined our vacation to go," Adrian said. "Sitting on the side of the road with a flat tire."

"Well, it could be worse," said Erica. "At least it's a nice day out. If it was raining, nobody would ever stop."

"That's fair," Adrian said. "But it doesn't really matter if there's nobody on the road, period."

"I'm sure someone will drive down eventually," Adrian's dad said as he was turning on the RV's hazard lights. "It might be a road in the middle of nowhere, but it's not abandoned."

"You think we could walk to the closest repair place?" Erica asked. "How far could it be?"

Adrian's mom looked up from the stove and said, "Well, without data connection, I can't look it up. And, besides, we're in the middle of nowhere. It's probably a pretty long walk."

"And there's no way we can replace the tire without a jack?" Adrian asked.

"You two, relax," Adrian's dad said, chuckling. "Being stuck with a flat tire isn't the worst thing in the world. Especially not in an RV with running water and electricity."

"Okay, you're right," Erica agreed. "But it's still unnerving. What did we hit, anyway?"

"I don't know," said Adrian's dad. "Probably a nail or something else sharp. I didn't see anything on the road, though."

"I'll look at the tire later," Adrian said. "At least, I will if nobody stops. Luckily this road is pretty empty, so there wasn't much of anything to hit when our tire blew."

"Wait, I think there's a car coming," Adrian's mom said suddenly, looking out the kitchen window. Sure enough, a blue pickup truck came into view, but instead of stopping at the RV, the driver instead sped right by them without even bothering to look.

"What a jerk!" Erica exclaimed. "He just completely ignored us."

"You'd be surprised how many don't bother to stop for cars on the shoulder," Adrian's mom said. "We can probably expect for more cars to pass us before one finally stops."

Erica sunk back in her chair. "Awesome," she said, sarcastically. "Also, where did Katie go?"

"I think that she went to sleep," said Adrian. "She didn't go to bed until late last night, and she gets really sleepy when we're driving."

Adrian's mom served everyone a plate a food and they all started eating while occasionally looking out the window are listening for the sound of a car approaching.

PHOEBE AND SCOTT TALKED for about an hour after McKinley and Miles left. They talked about what the officers had said, school, and just things that teenagers talked about in general. It was around 3pm when Scott stood up and said, "I should get going. I need to finish my homework before Monday."

Phoebe nodded. "Alright, I'll see you tomorrow at school," she said. "Be careful walking home."

"I'm sure I'll be fine," Scott said. "It's the middle of the day. If the thieves do intend to come after me, I doubt that they'll do it in broad daylight."

"I know, I know," Phoebe answered. "Just...be careful anyway."

"I will," Scott said, grabbing his backpack. After saying bye to Phoebe again, he headed back home.

Scott got home in about 20 minutes and without any incidents. After arriving home, he started his laptop and decided to finish his project. He worked on it for about half an hour, when he decided to take a break.

He headed down to the kitchen and grabbed himself a bag of trail mix off the top of the fridge. But before he got a chance to eat any of it, his phone started ringing. Scott put down the bag on trail mix and picked up his phone. It was Officer McKinley calling, but Scott didn't know why.

"Hello?" Scott asked. "What's the matter?"

"Scott," Officer McKinley responded. "There's something that you need to know."

"Okay..." Scott said. "What is it?"

"We showed a photo of the two thieves around the town," McKinley said. "Asked people if they had seen them around. It turns out that at least 7 different people have seen today."

"Which means?" Scott asked, not sure of what was coming.

"It means that Phoebe was correct," McKinley said. "Instead of leaving town, they're staying, which more than likely means that they're coming for Erica."

"But she's in Michigan," Scott protested.

"They don't know that," McKinley responded. "And they might try to get to her through one of you. So, I need you and Phoebe to both be watchful."

"How likely is it that they'll come after us?" Scott asked, concerned now.

"I don't know," said McKinley. "But we have to assume that the chances are high. And there's no sense in taking useless risks."

"So, can you put officers outside my house? And Phoebe's house?" Scott asked. "That would protect us, right?"

"Scott, we live in a small town," McKinley answered. "I only have 6 officers on duty, counting me and Officer Miles. I already have one outside your parents' store. If I place an officer outside Phoebe and your houses, that leaves me 1 officer to respond to any other calls."

"And besides," McKinley continued, "The thieves don't know where you or Phoebe live. If I place officers outside your houses, that basically just tells them exactly where you are. And I can't ask an officer to stand outside your houses for 24 hours a day."

"Okay, I get it," said Scott. "But what am I supposed to do?"

"Just do what I said before. Try to avoid walking places by yourself. And keep your phone handy. If you see one or both of the thieves, don't hesitate to call me."

"Okay," said Scott. "What about Phoebe? Did you tell her what you told me?"

"Officer Miles is telling her right now," McKinley answered. "Just relax for now. And remember what I told you."

"I will," Scott promised. After saying goodbye to Officer McKinley, he hung the phone up and thought about what McKinley had said.

He didn't want to admit it, but he was nervous. He saw what the thieves were capable of firsthand, and he didn't really want to experience it again. He decided that he might as well just go back to doing homework.

He hoped that it would put thoughts of the thieves out of his mind, and it did indeed do the job. Scott was able to finish his homework up and help his parents make dinner when they arrived home from the store.

It was around 9pm when Scott finally went to bed. He fell asleep quickly, despite his constant worries that the thieves would come after him at his home.

Phoebe was also experiencing similar thoughts. Officer Miles had just called her and given her the same news the McKinley had given Scott. She knew that she wasn't much of a fighter, so if the thieves did come after her, there wasn't much she could do.

So, to distract herself from the issue, she decided to do what she was doing in the first place: read. She grabbed her book from where she had left it and plopped back down on her bed.

She quickly got lost in her book and read for almost an hour straight, stopping only to greet her parents when they came home from work. Eventually, though, she had to put the book down to join her parents for dinner.

After dinner, Phoebe tried to go back to reading her book, while her parents went through the mail, but she was getting tired, so she instead decided that she might as well go to bed.

She said good night to her parents and headed off to bed. And, just like Scott, she was able to fall asleep easily, mostly because she managed to put the thieves in the back of her mind and instead think about the history presentation contest that was coming up in a few weeks.

BEFORE ANY OF THIS, though, Adrian's family and Erica were still stranded on the side of the road. It had been almost an hour after the pickup truck had sped by them and they were all starting to lose hope that anyone was going to stop to pick them up.

They all tried to pass the time by chatting, playing games, and basically just doing stuff to keep themselves occupied. Eventually, though, they all started to get bored and at 6pm, Erica said, "We've been here for almost 3 hours now and we've seen one car. I doubt that anyone is going to come down this road."

Katie had woken up from her nap by this time and she offered her solution. "Why doesn't Dad just lift the RV up? How heavy can it be?"

Adrian's dad laughed. "I don't think so, honey," he said. "Maybe if Adrian helped me, though."

Now Adrian laughed. Then his face turned serious and he asked, "Dad, what do we do if nobody comes by? We can't stay here all night."

"Technically, we can," Adrian's mom replied. "The generator should last up to 400 hours with the gas that we have left, and we have enough water in our tank for all of us to shower."

"Mom!" Adrian said. "You're not actually thinking of staying here, are you?"

"It's not the most...ideal solution, no," Adrian's mom said. "But we might have no choice."

"Dad, what's about the RV's built-in jacks?" Adrian asked. "Can we use those?"

The Curtis' RV had built-in jacks, but they were used for leveling out the RV if it was parked on a sloped ground, not for raising the RV off the ground.

"They're self-leveling, so I don't think so," Adrian's dad replied. "They'll stop when they level out the RV."

"But isn't there an override option?" Adrian asked.

"There is," Adrian's dad replied, pointing to a panel mounted above the couch. "But they weren't meant for that."

"But they could be used for that, right?" Adrian said.

"I suppose so, but it's probably dangerous," Adrian's dad answered. "And how would you go about doing it anyway?"

"Well, there's four jacks," Adrian started. "Two in the back and two in the front. All we have to do is raise up the two back jacks until the tires are off the ground. Then we can just put the spare tire on."

"I don't know if the back jacks can handle that much weight," said Erica, who had been listening to Adrian's idea.

"It's that, or we stay here all night," Adrian said. "Let's face it. This road is basically unused and nobody's going to be driving down it anytime soon."

"You're right," Adrian's mom said. "We could at least give it a try. But if the jacks start to give out, we're waiting until a car comes."

"Great," said Adrian, standing up and walking over to the panel. He was about to press the override button, but his dad stopped him.

"At least wait until we're all out of the RV first," he said. "The less weight in the RV, the better."

Adrian nodded, and everyone except for him climbed out of the RV. Adrian's dad grabbed the lug wrench from the compartment and Adrian hit the override button. A screen came up on the panel that allowed him to control the jacks manually.

Adrian started raising the back of the RV up and it didn't take long for the panel to start alerting him that the RV was becoming unbalanced. He kept raising the back up until Erica shouted from outside, "Okay, the tires are off the ground."

Adrian grabbed the spare tire from under the closet and lugged it outside. His Dad was working on removing the bolts and since he had already loosened them before they raised the RV up, they came off easily.

With Adrian's help, his dad managed to slide the tire off. Erica rolled the spare tire over to them and helped Adrian and his Dad slide the tire onto the axle. After they had slid the tire onto the axle, though, the jacks started to make creaking noises and they could see the strain that they were under.

Adrian rushed inside to lower the RV's jacks, and he managed to do so before they gave way. Adrian's dad screwed the bolts onto the tire and Adrian and Erica lugged the old tire into the RV.

Adrian's dad tightened the last bolt, and they all breathed a sigh of relief. "I cannot believe that worked," Adrian's dad said. "Hopefully we never have to do that again."

The rest of them agreed and they all climbed back into the RV. Adrian's dad started the RV, and pulled back onto the road.

"Obviously, this spare tire isn't going to get us all the way to Michigan, so we'll have to find a tire place that's close by," Adrian's dad said, as he started back down the road.

"Well, we still have no cell signal, so we'll have to get back on the highway first," Erica said. She pointed to a sign on the side of the road. "Which is apparently in about 10 miles."

Once they had gotten back on the highway, Adrian found a tire repair place that was still open, and Adrian's dad drove up to the place. The mechanic told them that he could patch the tire or replace it entirely.

Adrian's parents opted for the replacement, even though the mechanic told them that it would take longer. The mechanic said that he could have it finished by tomorrow morning, since he would have to have a tire sent over from their warehouse, so Adrian's dad decided that staying in a hotel would be the best option, rather than sleeping in the RV, which was parked in the mechanic's garage.

Adrian's parents found a hotel within walking distance, so they booked a night there. They booked 2 rooms, so the girls could have their own room and the boys could have theirs.

Everyone fell asleep quickly, since it had been quite the exhausting day. They'd get to Michigan a day late, but it was okay.

'At least we didn't have to spend a night on the side of the road,' Adrian thought to himself before he fell asleep.

SCOTT WOKE UP EARLY the next morning, but not as early as his parents. His parents would always wake up at around 5:30am, since they had to get the store open by 6. Scott made himself some breakfast, grabbed his backpack, and headed off to school.

He got there at around the same time as Phoebe, and met her in the parking lot.

As usual, Phoebe's bag was stuffed to the brim with books and school supplies, all for the many different classes she took.

"Someday you're going to collapse from all that weight," Scott said, shaking his head.

"It's really not that heavy," Phoebe said, swinging the backpack off her shoulder as she walked into school. She handed it to Scott who picked it up by the handle, and immediately dropped it.

"Not heavy?" Scott asked. "That thing feels like a stack of bricks."

"No, you're just weak," Phoebe said, picking her backpack up as the school bell rang and they headed off to their classes.

Classes went smoothly for both of them, but Scott did have to admit that it was strange, not seeing Adrian, or Erica in the hall. It was rare for two of them to not show up to school at the same time.

Lunch, Scott's favorite class, was right after P.E. He headed off to his hallway locker to get his change of clothes and changed in the boy's locker room. After he had finished changing, though, he noticed that he didn't have his wallet.

'Must've left it in my locker,' Scott thought, as he searched the pockets of his clothes. 'I'll grab it when I put my gym clothes away.'

But when Scott got to his locker, he couldn't find his wallet anyway. Worried now, he searched all his pockets again, and then the pockets of his gym clothes, but it was nowhere to be found. He stuck his head into his locker and started rummaging through everything it, hoping his wallet had just gotten buried.

"Uh, Scott, lunch is starting soon," a voice from behind him said. It was Phoebe, and she was watching Scott dig through his locker.

"Phoebe," Scott asked, "Have you seen my wallet anywhere?"

"Your wallet?" Phoebe repeated. "No, isn't it in your locker?"

"I swear I put it in there, but I can't find it anywhere," Scott said. "And it's not in any of my pockets either."

"Are you sure you brought it to school with you?" Phoebe asked. "You might have left it home."

"No, my school ID is in there," Scott said. "I just had it before P.E. I *know* I put it in my locker."

"Did you lock your locker?" Phoebe asked.

"I have a padlock on it," Scott said. "And the key is right here." He dug a keychain out of his pocket.

"I don't know, Scott," Phoebe said. "Maybe you just dropped it somewhere."

"Maybe..." Scott said. But he didn't sound convinced.

"Lunch is starting in about 2 minutes, so I'll meet you there," Phoebe said, heading back down the hallway. Scott started putting things back in his locker and racking his brain, thinking of what he could have done with his wallet.

He met up with Phoebe in the back of the lunch line, but he quickly realized something.

"Shoot, I can't pay for lunch," Scott said. "All my money is in my wallet."

"It's fine, I'll pay for you," Phoebe said, handing Scott a five-dollar bill. "Don't worry about paying me back."

"Thanks," Scott said. "Are you sure you don't want me to pay you back?"

"Trust me," Phoebe said. "It's perfectly fine."

"Okay then," Scott said, gazing around the room. "I-" He suddenly stopped talking and tapped Phoebe on the shoulder. "Look," he said, pointing to a girl with dark hair, who was paying for her lunch at the front of the line.

"What?" Phoebe asked. "Why are you pointing at that girl?"

"She's holding my wallet!" Scott said. The girl was indeed pulling cash out of a wallet, but Phoebe couldn't tell if it was Scott's or not.

"How can you tell?" Phoebe asked. "It could just be a wallet that looks like yours."

"No, it's my wallet," Scott said, inching forward in the line. "Look at that sticker on the cover." He pointed to a Spider-Man sticker on the cover of the wallet.

"I put that sticker there about a year ago," Scott said. "And what girl would have a spider-man sticker on their wallet?"

Scott watched as the girl grabbed a school lunch tray and headed over to a table to sit down. "Hold my spot in line," Scott told Phoebe and walked over to the table where the girl was sitting.

Scott stood at the front of the table, but the girl didn't notice him, so Scott cleared his throat loudly. The girl looked up from her meal and asked, "Can I help you?"

"I believe you have something that belongs to me," Scott said, annoyed.

The girl asked. "What are you talking about?"

"Oh please," Scott said, irritated. "I just watched you take out *my* wallet and pay for your lunch."

The girl shook her head. "You must have me confused with someone else. I paid for this with my own money."

"Stop lying," Scott said. "I know you have my wallet." He reached down and tried to pull his wallet out of her pocket. The girl punched him in the stomach, knocking the wind out of him.

"Hey, keep your hands to yourself, dummy," the girl answered. "I don't have your wallet, so go away and let me eat in peace."

Breathing hard, Scott shook his head. "If you don't give me back my wallet, I'll tell Principal Peterson that I saw you with my wallet."

Instead of giving Scott back his wallet, the girl laughed. "*That's* your best threat? Tell the principal. You don't even have any proof that I stole it. You gotta do better than that."

Scott sighed and took a seat next to the girl. "Just give me back my wallet," he said. "Honestly, I won't even tell Principal Peterson if you give it back."

"I don't have your wallet, okay," the girl said. "Go away before I punch you in the stomach again."

Someone cleared their throat loudly behind Scott and the girl, and they both whirled around. It was Phoebe, and she was holding Scott's wallet.

"You don't have Scott's wallet anymore," Phoebe said. "So that makes your last sentence the only true thing that you said."

"Where did you get that?!" the girl asked, trying to grab it from Phoebe. Phoebe pulled her arm back, and said "From your pocket."

"My pocket?" the girl asked. "How did you get it out without me noticing?"

"That's not important," Phoebe said, walking over to Scott and handing him his wallet. "But you should work on making things in your pocket less conspicuous."

"And now, I do have proof that you stole my wallet," Scott said. "So, let's see you laugh about my telling the principal now."

"You're such a dork," the girl said. "And you're the textbook example of a nerd." She pointed at Phoebe.

"Really not helping your case," Scott said.

"Alright, look, sure, I stole your wallet," the girl said. "But it was just a harmless prank, right?"

"Prank!" Scott said. "You used it to pay for your lunch. Which means that you owe me five dollars."

"I don't have five dollars, okay," the girl said. "Why do you think I stole your wallet?"

It was now that Scott noticed that the girl was wearing very worn-out and old clothes, her hair was tangled and messy, and her hands were dirty and cut.

"Look, I know I laughed about it at first, but you can't tell Principal Peterson about this," the girl said.

"I'm really not seeing a reason not to," Scott said. "I mean, you broke into my locker and stole my wallet."

"I already have two strikes," the girl said. "If I get a third strike, I'm going to get expelled, and my parents will kill me if I get expelled."

Scott sighed. "How did you get into my locker anyway?" he asked.

"Picked the lock," the girl replied. "It's really not that hard and your lock was cheapy."

"Seriously? I paid 20 bucks for that lock," Scott said incredulously. "Fine, I won't tell Principal Peterson, but you have to stop stealing stuff."

"What do you want?" the girl asked. "I can't afford lunch, and I'm not going to starve all day."

"What about your parents?" Phoebe broke in. "Wouldn't they give you money for school lunch?"

The girl snorted. "Forget my parents. My dad is drunk half the time, and if you ask him for money, he loses it. And my mom is pretty much never home, but nobody knows where she goes."

Scott and Phoebe didn't know what to say. "That's...awful," said Scott. "You don't have relatives or anything that you could stay with?"

"My grandparents all died before I was born, and all my other relatives live halfway across the country," the girl answered. "Look, not everybody's life is picture-perfect, but I make the best I can out of it by picking up skills that help me get around."

"What's your name?" Scott asked. "And how old are you?"

"Remington," the girl replied. "I'm 14. Listen, I'm sorry about your wallet, but I do what I have to do to get money, even if it means stealing."

"What about getting a job?" Phoebe asked.

"What, you think stealing was my first choice?" Remington said. "No, I've tried to get a job before. But my dad has a really bad reputation in this town, and nobody wants to hire his daughter."

"What do you mean by 'bad reputation'?" Scott asked.

"Well, he's been arrested like 10 times for stupid things, like getting into fights while he's drunk, DUI's and other small crimes," Remington responded. "So, I guess people think I'm going to be just like him, so they won't hire me."

"Well, that's not fair or right," Scott said.

"Yeah, well, that's why I end up having to steal money. It's that, or skip lunch," Remington said.

"So, if you could get a job, would you take it?" Scott asked.

"Of course," Remington said. "I don't want to steal; I just don't have a choice. Why?"

"Well, my parents own a store, and they always need extra help," Scott said. "I could probably get you a job there, if you're interested."

"Are you kidding?" Remington asked. "That would be great. Honestly, the less time I spend at home, the better."

"Well, I can't promise, but I'll ask my parents," Scott said. The school bell started to ring, and Scott said, "I'll meet you after school and talk to you about it. And you can forget about the five dollars, but don't call me a dork again." He stuck his wallet in his pocket and headed back to class with Phoebe.

Chapter IV

Adrian's family and Erica were finally back on the road again. They had picked up the RV early Monday morning, and Adrian's dad didn't waste any time getting back on the road, hoping to get to the campsite by nighttime.

"So, how long until we get to the campsite?" Erica asked.

"According to the GPS, not for another 8 hours," Adrian said. "We should get there by 6pm."

"Ooh, fun," Erica said. "Of course, that assumes the we won't get another flat tire."

"Hey, don't jinx us," Adrian's dad said, looking over from the front seat. "We'll probably get to the campsite closer to 7pm, not 6pm, since there's always traffic on this route.

"In the meantime," Katie said, "Would anyone like to play Monopoly." She plopped a worn-out looking Monopoly box on the table.

Erica looked at the box. "How old is this?" she asked.

"We've had it before I was born," Adrian said. "I think it was used to be my Dad's when he was a kid."

Erica raised her eyebrows. "Wow, okay. I'm impressed that it still has all the pieces."

"Oh, it doesn't," Katie said. "Half the player pieces are missing, and a bunch of the property cards are missing as well."

"Uh, okay," said Erica. "That will make it hard to play."

Adrian shook his head and got up from the table. He came back shortly holding another monopoly box, but this one looked a lot newer.

"This one has all the pieces," Adrian said. "It was my birthday present, so Katie's not allowed to play it without me."

"Why did you bring the old Monopoly box with you?" Erica asked. "If you have the new one."

"Katie brought it," Adrian said, setting up the Monopoly board. "What piece do you want to be?"

"Ship, please," said Erica.

"Okay, I'll be the car," Adrian said. "Mom, want to join?"

Adrian's mom looked over from the book she was reading. "No, that's okay. You three have fun."

"Okay then," Adrian said. "Katie, what piece do you want to be?"

"The puppy, of course," Katie said, grabbing the piece out of the box.

The three of them played Monopoly for about 2 hours before Adrian finally bankrupted Erica when she landed on Boardwalk.

"Okay, that was not fair," Erica protested. "Why did you get all of Katie's properties?"

"Because I bankrupted her," Adrian said, folding the board up and putting it in the box. "That's the rules. If I bankrupt Katie, I get her properties. If you had bankrupted Katie, you would've gotten her properties."

"Okay, but shouldn't you only get enough properties to cover Katie's debt?" Erica asked. "Why all of them?"

"I didn't make the rules," Adrian said. "That's just how it is."

"Fine, but I want a rematch someday," Erica said. "You haven't seen my true Monopoly skills yet."

Adrian laughed. "So, not only are you great at sports, you're great at board games?"

"No, just Monopoly," Erica said, laughing. She got up from the table and stretched her legs. "You know, I've never been on a drive this long before."

"Never?" Adrian asked. "Don't you ever go on vacation?"

"Sure," Erica said. "Just not usually this far. We normally only travel a few hours."

"Trust me, it's a great experience to be this far from home," Adrian said. "Although, the long drives do get rather dull after a while."

"So, once we get to Michigan, what are we going to do?" Erica asked. "Do we have a plan or anything?"

"Not really," Adrian said. "For most vacations, we do whatever. Probably just see what's nearby and check out some of the attractions."

"Sounds fun," Erica said. "What else can we do for the remaining 6-hour drive?"

"More board games," Adrian suggested. "But other than that, not much."

"I could go for some lunch," Erica said. "Do we have anything to eat?"

"Check the fridge," Adrian said. "We probably have some fruit or something. Or if you want to cook something up, you can probably do that too."

"Not while the RV's moving," Erica said. "That seems dangerous."

"We're on the highway and we probably will be for another few hours," Adrian said. "You'll be fine, just don't cook up soup or anything."

"I think I'll stick with fruit," Erica said, grabbing an orange from the fridge. She leaned back in her chair and sighed. "Only 6 more hours on the road."

SCHOOL FINALLY ENDED for Scott and Phoebe after what felt like an eternity. After grabbing his backpack, Scott headed for the exit and ran into Remington standing near the door.

"Remington, hi," Scott said. "Are you still interested in the job at my parents' store?"

Remington nodded. "Of course. You said to meet you after school and you'd tell me more about it."

"Yeah, no problem," Scott said. "I-" He stopped talking when he noticed Phoebe standing in the hallway and waving him over. "Give me a second," he said, holding up a finger.

Remington nodded and Scott walked over to Phoebe. "What's the matter?" he asked.

"Nothing, I just wanted to ask you," Phoebe said. "Are you sure it's a good idea to have Remington work at your parents' store?"

"What do you mean?" Scott asked.

"She's a thief, Scott!" Phoebe said. "And who knows what else. I mean, who's to say that she won't rob your parents' store?"

"Phoebe, seriously?" Scott asked. "I'm sure that she'll be fine. Didn't you hear her, anyway? She said that she only steals because she can't get a job."

"Scott, she could have been lying," Phoebe said. "Look, I don't want to put down somebody else, but I think that you trust people too easily."

"Or maybe you're too distrustful," Scott said.

"Well, if that's how you feel about it," Phoebe said, insulted. "Don't blame me if she empties the cash register when you're not looking."

"Phoebe-" Scott started.

"Forget it," Phoebe said, grabbing her backpack and walking away in the opposite direction.

Scott sighed and walked back over to Remington who was still standing at the doorway.

"What was that about?" she asked.

"Nothing," Scott said. "Just some silly disagreement. Anyway, I texted my parents about you and asked if they needed some extra help."

"And?" Remington asked. "What did they say?"

"They said that they'd be interested in meeting you," Scott said, walking out of the parking lot. "And that they'd certainly be open to the idea of giving you a job."

Remington followed Scott out to the road. "How big is your parent's store?" she asked.

"Here, follow me," Scott said. "Their store isn't that far from the school, and it'll give you a chance to meet them."

Remington followed Scott down a couple of roads, when suddenly a small, grey car drove by them and tossed something out the window. Scott heard the sound of metal hitting asphalt, and then a blinding light completely obscured his vision.

Scott couldn't see anything, but suddenly he felt hands grabbing his arms. He tried to fight them off, but he felt something hit the back of his head, and then everything went black.

Scott woke up in a dark room. The back of his head ached, and he had no idea how long it had been since he was unconscious. His vision was still blurry, but he was able to make out the shape of two men walking towards him.

Scott blinked and his vision got clearer. The lights in the room turned on, and Scott could tell that he was in some sort of factory. In fact, the place seemed vaguely familiar.

"Hello Scott," one of the men said, stepping forward. Scott recognized the voice to be one of the thieves who had kidnapped Erica before and now escaped from prison.

"How do you know my name?" Scott asked. One of the men tossed Scott's wallet at his feet, but Scott's arms were tied behind his back, so he was unable to pick it up.

"We know your address as well," the man said, showing Scott his school ID. It had his DOB, address, picture, and full name on it.

"Scott William Ryder," the man read aloud. "It's got a nice ring to it, doesn't it?"

"What do you want from me?" Scott asked. "What's this about?"

"Oh, we just want to know where one Erica Feldman is," the other man said. "You wouldn't happen to know her, would you?"

"You planned a prison breakout and risked coming after me, just so you could get your revenge on a 15-year-old girl?" Scott asked. "That's pathetic."

One of the men's fists smashed into Scott's face, causing him to wince in pain. "We're not here for revenge," the man said. "This is a lot deeper than you realize."

"Too bad," Scott said. "I'm not telling you where she is."

Another fist smashed into Scott's face, this time causing his nose to bleed. "Come on, Scott," the other man said. "It's just some simple information. We know she went on vacation to Michigan. We just need to know where she's staying."

"Why would I tell you that?" Scott asked.

"Because..." one of the men said, drawing a large knife from the table behind him.

"Don't be ridiculous," Scott said. "You're not going to kill me."

"And just how can you be so certain of that?" the man holding the knife asked.

"Because if you kill me, you'll have no way of figuring out where Erica is," Scott replied.

"Maybe not, but trust me, eventually you'll tell us," the other man said.

"You can't keep me here forever," Scott said. "Eventually, someone will notice I'm missing."

"Oh, don't worry," the man with the knife said. "It'll take less than an hour to get you to talk."

"Don't count on it," Scott said. "I've been electrocuted, hit by a car, and gassed. There's not much more that you can do to me."

Suddenly there was a shattering of glass and a loud bang from the room next door. The two men looked at each other and headed off into the room to check on it, leaving Scott alone.

Unsure of what to do now, Scott struggled with the ropes binding his hands, but they were too tight. He leaned back in his chair and tried to listen to what was going on in the other room.

"Psst, Scott." A voice from over in the corner caught Scott's attention. He turned to face the corner and saw Remington standing there.

"Remington!? What are you doing here?" Scott asked.

"What do you think?" Remington asked. She quickly walked over to Scott and flicked out a pocket knife. She sliced through the ropes that bound Scott to the chair and pulled him up from the chair.

"We gotta go," Remington said. "I tossed a smoke bomb through the window of the other room, but it won't take them long to come back in here."

She grabbed Scott's arm and yanked him towards the exit. "Wait, how are we going to get out of here?" Scott asked, reaching down and grabbing his wallet off the floor.

"I got that covered," Remington said, opening the exit door and pulling Scott outside "C'mon, hurry up," she said. "I don't know who those men are, but they look dangerous."

Scott followed Remington down the dirt path leading away from the warehouse until they saw a motorcycle leaning up against a tree.

"No way," said Scott. "You drive a *motorcycle*?"

"Yeah, there's a lot of things you don't know about me," Remington said, jumping on the motorcycle. "Are you getting on or not?"

Scott heard rapid footsteps approaching them, so he quickly hopped on the motorcycle seat behind Remington as she started the engine. Remington peeled away from the tree just as the two men came into view. Even over the sound of the motorcycle engine, Scott could hear them cursing at them.

"They're going to follow us!" Scott yelled over the sound of the engine. He had never ridden on a motorcycle before, and he had to say. It probably would have been an amazing experience if they weren't escaping from two potential murderers right now.

"I know!" Remington yelled back. "How far is your home?"

"I don't even know where we are!" Scott yelled. "And besides, we can't go to my home. They know where I live."

"Alright, we'll go to my house!" Remington replied, turning down a sharp corner. "It's not that far from here."

Remington drove the motorcycle another few miles down the road, when Scott suddenly turned around and noticed a car approaching them at a high speed.

"Remington!" Scott yelled, tapping her on the shoulder. "I think they're following us." The car was increasing speed and Scott guessed that it wouldn't be long before it caught up to them.

Remington looked behind her and yelled, "Hang on tight!" She pushed the throttle up and the motorcycle shot forward, almost causing Scott to fly off the motorcycle. He grabbed hold of the seat and gripped it for dear life.

"What are you doing?!" Scott asked, thinking that he was either going to fall off the motorcycle or get rammed into by the car behind them.

"I'm trying to lose them!" Remington shouted, turning another corner at almost 80mph. "We live in the middle of nowhere, so there's probably no other cars coming down."

Scott hung on to the seat as tight as he could, while Remington turned corner after corner, almost burning out the tires.

"Are they still behind us?!" Remington yelled to Scott.

Scott hesitantly looked behind him, but didn't see the car anymore. "I think you lost them," he yelled back.

"Great!" Remington yelled, turning another corner, almost throwing Scott off the motorcycle. She headed down the road for about a minute, when they came to a dingy looking trailer with trash all over the front lawn. Remington killed the engine and said, "We're here."

Scott got down off the motorcycle and looked around. "You live here?" he asked.

"I told you," Remington said, leaning the motorcycle against a tree. "We don't have a lot of money, so we don't live in a fancy house or anything."

She grabbed the keys out of the motorcycle and walked towards the door. "Come on," she said to Scott. "Get inside before they drive by and see you."

Scott followed Remington inside, and immediately noticed that the inside of the house wasn't much better than the outside. "My parents aren't home," Remington said, shoving stuff aside to clear a path to her room. "They probably won't be home until late, but they hate having visitors, so I can't let them know that you were here."

"I have so many questions," Scott said. "Starting with, how did you find me?"

"After we got flash-banged, I tossed a tracker onto the car that the two men were driving," Remington said. "I was able to trace it to the warehouse where you were."

"Why didn't you just tell the police or something?" Scott asked. "Wouldn't that have been a much better idea?"

"I...don't exactly get along too well with the police," Remington. "I try to avoid them as best I can."

"And how do you own a motorcycle?" Scott asked. "I don't think a 14-year old can legally own a motorcycle."

"It's my Dad's," Remington said. "I learned how to ride it a few years ago, and he never rides it anymore. Now you owe me an explanation. Who were those men and what did they want with you?"

"It's a long story," Scott said.

"Hey, I might have just saved your life," Remington said. "I think that at least I'm entitled to an explanation."

Scott sighed. "Okay, fine," he said. "But afterwards, we're calling Officer McKinley and telling him what happened."

"Deal," Remington said, taking a seat on her bed.

Scott took a seat on an empty chair and started the story. He started at Erica's kidnapping, and went through all the events and things that had happened to them in the past few weeks, ending with what had just happened.

"Okay, let me get this straight," Remington said. "These two nutjobs kidnapped your friend, Erica, and instead of booking it out of the country after escaping, they came after to you to figure out where she is?"

"Pretty much," Scott said. "One of them said that 'this was a lot deeper than I thought', but I don't know what he meant exactly."

Remington shook her head. "Geez. Now I feel bad for stealing your wallet."

"It's fine," Scott said. "Listen, we need to get out of here. Where's your phone? I'm going to call Officer McKinley."

"We...don't have a phone," Remington said.

"Okay, great," Scott said. Do you have a cell phone?"

"Sure," Remington said. "But there's no cell signal here. Believe me, I've tried."

"You don't have WiFi or anything?" Scott asked. When Remington shook her head, Scott asked "How do you get your homework done?"

"I go to the library," Remington said. "I told you: The less time I spend at home, the better."

"Well, this is great," Scott said. "At any minute, the thieves could find us, and then we'll just be sitting ducks."

"What about your phone?" Remington asked. "Do you have cell signal?"

"The thieves took all my stuff when they kidnapped me," Scott said. "My backpack and phone are back in the warehouse. The only thing I have is my wallet."

Scott and Remington sat in silence for a while, trying to formulate a plan that would get them out of this predicament, but nothing came to mind. Finally, Scott said, "We can't just sit here forever. Do any of your neighbors have phones?"

Remington shrugged. "No idea. Honestly, I try to stay away from my neighbors. They're pretty unsavory people."

"Well, there has to be something that we can do," Scott said. "How long has it been since we were attacked?"

Remington glanced at a clock. "A few hours," she said. "Look, why don't we just make a run- "

Remington was interrupted by a loud pounding at the front door. Scott and Remington turned to look at each other, both dreading who it could be.

"Would your parents be home by now?" Scott asked quietly.

Remington shook her head. "No, and I never get visitors. It has to be them, but how did they find us. I could've-" Remington stopped, then looked at Scott in horror. "The motorcycle! I forgot to park it behind the house."

The pounding at the door continued, but this time it was followed by a voice shouting, "I know you're in there! You can't hide forever."

"It's them alright," Scott whispered. "What do we do?"

"What can we do?" Remington asked. "That door won't hold forever. And there's not a lot of places to hide in this house."

"Do you have any weapons?" Scott asked. "Something that we can use to defend ourselves?"

There were more bangs on the front door and Scott could hear it starting to give way.

Remington shook her head in response to Scott's question. "No, just kitchen knives and my pocket knife. We- Wait, my dad has a shotgun," she said. "But it's locked in his gun safe and I don't know the combination."

"I thought you knew how to pick locks!" Scott said.

"Not that kind of lock," Remington said. "Just locks with keyholes. I don't think it's even possible to pick a combination lock."

More bangs. "Well, we have to do something!" Scott said. "Once that door gives way, we're toast. Where's your Dad's gun cabinet?"

Remington led Scott to the back of the house where her dad kept his shotgun. The case was made out of plexiglass with a metal frame, designed to be both water and fire resistant.

"My dad spent a couple hundred on this," Remington said. "He and my Mom fought about it for months. There's no way we're going to get into this."

"You're sure you have no idea what the combination is?" Scott asked. "Your dad has never mentioned it before?"

"I don't know, okay!" Remington said. "Look-" Remington was interrupted by the sound of the door crashing in, and her eyes grew wide. The sound of the two men racing through the house could be heard even in the back of the house.

Remington grabbed Scott's arm and said, "We need to go to my parents' bedroom! My dad has a deadbolt lock on the door. It should hold them off for a while."

Remington and Scott dashed through the house and made it to the bedroom, just as the men spotted them. Scott dove into the bedroom and slammed the door

as one the men grabbed Remington and pulled her away from the bedroom.

"Come on out, Scott!" one of the men said tauntingly. "We have your girlfriend. You have exactly 1 minute to step out of that room or we'll put a bullet in her head."

"Scott, don't do it!" Remington shouted. "It's-ouch!" One of the men had slammed Remington into a wall, creating a gash in the back of her head.

"40 seconds, Scott," the man said. "40 seconds before she and you both die."

Scott desperately dug through all the drawers in the dresser and night-table for something useful, but there was nothing."

"30 seconds!" the man yelled. "Don't make this harder than it needs to be, Scott!"

"Scott!" Remington shouted. "Forget about me. The window-". Remington uttered a shriek of pain as the man holding her twisted her arm, hard. "Shut up," the man growled, not letting his grip on her arm loosen.

Scott looked at the window. He knew what Remington was trying to tell him: escape through the window, but he wasn't about to leave Remington to get murdered.

"20 seconds!" the man shouted. "Clock's counting down, Scott. It's not a difficult choice."

Scott dug through one of the desk drawers, hoping just to find something, whether it be a gun, knife, or even just a box opener, but it was all just pens, pencils, and tissues.

"Come on, Scott. 10 seconds left," the man outside said. "Are you really going to let this girl die because of you?"

Scott dug through the last drawer in the desk, but there was no knives or guns to be found. Instead, the only thing in the desk was a piece of paper.

"Five, Four, Three, Two," the man raised his gun to Remington's head. "Last chance, Scott!"

Scott grabbed the piece of paper and balled it up in his fist.

"One!" The man was about to pull the trigger when Scott swung the door open. "Wait!" he shouted. The man lowered the gun away from Remington's head. "Don't shoot her!" Scott said. "You can have me, just let her go."

"Ah, wise decision, Scott," the man holding Remington said. He let go of Remington's arm, causing her to wince in pain. He shoved Remington to the ground and the other man pointed his gun at Scott. Scott raised his hands in surrender, while subtlety dropping the paper in his hand on the ground near Remington, praying that she would notice.

The man jabbed the gun into Scott's back and said, "Walk." Scott obediently walked towards the door, slowly as Remington stood up. Scott tried to signal to Remington to pick the paper up with his eyes, but she had already noticed it. She picked it up and dashed off.

Scott sighed. "Walk faster," the man growled. Scott quickened his pace a little, and just as they reached the front door, the click of a shotgun could be heard from behind them.

"Let him go, turn around slowly, and put your guns on the ground," Remington said steely. "Reach for the trigger and I'll blow both of you away."

The man let go of Scott and both of the put their guns on the ground. "You're making a mistake," one of them said. "There's no need for you to get involved in this. If you put down the shotgun and walk away, we'll forget you ever existed.

"Shut up," Remington said, cocking the shotgun. "Turn around and face me. Scott, can you pick up their pistols?"

Scott grabbed the pistols off the ground as the two men turned to face Remington. As he picked up the second pistol, one of the men suddenly grabbed a knife from his pocket and lunged at Remington.

There was a loud blast, a yell of pain, and Remington was holding a smoking shotgun, while the man was on the ground holding his leg.

"I warned you," Remington said. "You come at me again, and I'll blast your other leg."

Scott grabbed the second pistol off the ground and pointed it at the man who was still standing. "Remington," he said. "Can you watch these two while I go and find a phone and call Officer McKinley."

Remington nodded. "Don't worry. These two aren't going anywhere."

Scott handed Remington one of the pistols and borrowed her cell phone. He took off running down the road until he finally found a place where there was cell signal. He dialed Officer McKinley's number and he picked up on the first ring.

"Scott, what can I do for you?" he asked.

As fast as he could and in between breaths, Scott explained everything that had happened to him and Remington and told Officer McKinley where to find them.

"Okay, I'll be there in a few minutes," McKinley said. "Just make sure that they don't go anywhere."

"Remington's got that covered," Scott said. "I'll see you shortly." He hung up the phone and ran back to the house.

As soon as he reached the house, he noticed that something was wrong. The door was left open, and he knew that he had closed it. He grabbed the gun that he had taken from the men out of his pocket and slowly made his way into the house.

The man who Remington had shot was still lying on the ground, but Remington and the other man were gone. The shotgun that she had been holding was lying on the ground, next to a puddle of what looked like blood.

"Remington!" Scott shouted. "Where are you?" The man lying on the ground laughed painfully. "I warned you two to stay out of it," the man said.

Scott ran over to the man and pointed the gun at him. "Where's Remington?" he demanded. "What happened and where did they go?"

The man shrugged. "I don't know what you're talking about."

Scott kicked the man in the leg where Remington had shot him and the man yelled in pain. "Where did they go?!"

"I told you," the man said, wincing. "This is much deeper than you realize."

The sound of a police siren filled the air and Officer McKinley pulled up to the front door with his lights flashing.

"Scott, what's going on?" McKinley asked, rushing into the room, followed by Officer Miles. "Where's the second thief? And where's Remington?"

"I don't know, I don't know!" Scott said. "They were about 20 minutes ago when I left to go call you. I don't understand how they could have gotten away. Remington had them both at gunpoint."

McKinley looked at the man on the ground. "Why'd they leave you?" he demanded.

The man spat and said, "I know my rights. I don't have to say anything to you without a lawyer."

Officer Miles grabbed the man up by his arm, causing him to wince in pain again. "He needs a hospital," Miles said. "The ambulance should be here any minute."

"Scott, you need to tell me exactly what happened," McKinley said. "Detail by detail."

"We need to find Remington," Scott said. "Where did they take her?"

"Scott, calm down," McKinley said. "We will find her, but right now, we just need to know what happened."

Scott took a deep breath. "Okay, I'll explain everything." he said. "But we need to find Remington before the thieves kill her."

Chapter V

After Scott had left to make the phone call to McKinley, Remington stood guard, making sure that neither of the thieves moved a muscle. She kept her shotgun focused on the thief who was still standing up, making sure not to take his eyes off of him.

"You don't know what you're doing at all," the man said.

"So, you've told me," Remington responded. "It doesn't take a genius to figure this out, though."

"Think about it this way," the man said. "There's no reason for you to involved. You don't even know either of us, and you just met Scott."

"I don't know how you know that," Remington said, "But you got me involved when you slammed my head against a wall."

The gash in the back of Remington's head had started to sting, causing her to wince. She felt the gash and felt fresh blood. It wasn't the worst injury that she had sustained in her life, though.

However, the pain from the gash was enough of a distraction for Remington to take her eyes off of the two men for a few seconds. In a split second, the man standing had grabbed a knife from his pocket and launched it at Remington.

The knife buried itself in Remington's arm, causing her to drop the shotgun. The man seized the opportunity and tackled Remington to the ground, grabbing his pistol back from her.

He pointed it at Remington and said, "Stand up."

Everything was spinning. Remington could barely see straight from the pain the knife in her arm was causing. The knife had obviously hit a nerve in her arm. She barely heard what the man had said to her.

"Stand up!" the man shouted, grabbing Remington and pulling her up. Remington was still dizzy though, and as she was being forced towards the door, she couldn't take it anymore and her body collapsed.

The man dragged Remington to the car outside and tossed her into the back seat, then sped away, leaving the man inside behind.

The man drove for about 20 minutes, but Remington was unconscious for the entire ride, so she had no idea where they were going. She didn't wake up until the man dragged her inside a building and dumped a bucket of ice water on her head.

Remington gasped and sputtered. The knife was still in her arm, but she didn't feel the pain as much anymore. The cut on the back of her head was becoming more painful every minute, though.

"How much do you know?" the man demanded of Remington.

"Know what?" Remington asked. The room wasn't spinning anymore, but she still felt dizzy. Sitting down made things easier, though.

The man grabbed the handle of the knife in Remington's arm and lightly twisted it, causing Remington to gasp in pain. Tears started to come to her eyes.

"Stop, please!" she begged. "I swear, I don't know what you're talking about."

The man twisted it harder and Remington screamed in pain. "Stop, stop! I swear, I don't know anything. Just what Scott told me."

The man let go of the knife, causing Remington's arm to drop limply. She couldn't feel her arm at all now, but at least it was better than the blinding pain it was causing before.

"And what exactly did Scott tell you?" the man demanded.

"Just that you guys were thieves," she said. "He said that you forced his friend to rob houses for you and that you pawned the stolen goods."

"And that's it?" the man asked, grabbing Remington's arm again. "You're sure?"

"Yes, yes, I swear!" Remington said hastily. The cut in her head was throbbing now and the room was starting to spin again.

The man sighed, but whether in relief or frustration, Remington couldn't tell. "How did you find us?" he demanded.

Remington didn't want to answer the question, since she knew it was the only way that Scott and Officer McKinley would be able to find them. "Lucky guess," she said.

This time the man actually chuckled. "I admire your bravery," he said. "You would have actually made a much better partner than that last girl."

"She wasn't your partner," Remington said. "You forced her to rob for you."

"Well, I did what I had to do," the man said. "You shot my actual partner with a shotgun, so you've really put a hole in my plans."

"What plans? Burglary?" Remington asked.

"Oh, this isn't about burglary," the man said. "Those first two houses were just a test. Until the real challenge came alone."

"What real challenge?" Remington asked.

"I'm not stupid," the man said. "Now, let me ask you again? How did you find us?"

"I told you, it was a lucky guess," Remington said.

The man looked at the knife that was still in Remington's arm. "Do you want me to twist that again?"

Remington gulped. Then again, she couldn't feel her arm anyway, so she figured that she probably wouldn't feel the pain. She shrugged. "No, but you're going to anyway, aren't you?" she said.

The man walked closer to Remington. "Not if you tell me the truth."

"What, you don't believe that I could've guessed so accurately?" Remington said. "I'll have you know that I'm a master of card games." The pain in her arm was gone and she had gotten used to the pain from the gash in her head, so Remington was able to think clearly again.

"Don't play the hero here," the man said, grabbing the knife in his hand. But Remington didn't feel anything. In fact, she didn't even feel anything when the man twisted the knife. Maybe a small stinging, but other than that, it was completely numb.

The man was distracted, so Remington took advantage of that. Since she wasn't tied to the chair, she lifted her leg, and kicked the man in the stomach. The man grunted, stunned and out of breath.

Remington stood up and was about to launch another kick at the man, but she couldn't keep her balance because of the dizziness and collapsed again. The man stood up and dragged Remington back onto the chair, this time making sure to tie both her arms and legs to it.

He shook her a couple of times, trying to wake her up, but she didn't respond. She didn't revive even when he dumped the remainder of the ice water on her. Frustrated, he starting rummaging through a duffel bag that he had taken from the car, looking for something.

SCOTT WAS GIVING MCKINLEY all the details of what had happened, as best as he could remember. He had gotten up to the part about Remington finding him in the warehouse when he remembered something important.

"Officer McKinley!" Scott said suddenly. "I just remembered. Remington attached a tracker to the thieves' car. That's how she found me in the first place."

McKinley immediately knew what Scott was thinking. If the thief had taken Remington away in the same car that they had used to kidnap Scott, they might be able to track down the location of it, and hopefully find Remington.

"What kind of tracker did she use?" McKinley asked.

"I don't know," Scott said. "But I still have her phone. She might have used that to connect to the tracker."

He handed the phone over to McKinley who pulled the car over to the side of the road.

"Good, it's not locked," McKinley said, turning the phone on. He swiped through all of Remington's app before he found an app that looked like it might be used for a tracker.

He opened the app, and a map popped up with a little bubble on it. McKinley zoomed it and noticed that the bubble was located in an abandoned building, off a small, deserted road.

"The thief has to be there!" Scott said. "What's the address?"

McKinley zoomed in even farther until the building's address popped up. He plugged the address into the police car's GPS system, and they tore down the road.

THE MAN GRABBED A SMALL device from the duffel bag and pressed it against Remington's arm. The device sent a short electrical signal through Remington's body, which jolted her awake.

"Good, you're finally awake," the man said, tossing the device back into the bag. "Now answer the question. *How did you find me?*"

Remington's head was cloudy, and she couldn't see straight. She was vaguely aware of the man standing in front of her, but she couldn't understand anything he was saying.

"Answer me!" the man shouted, slapping Remington across the cheek. The stinging pain only made things worse, and she couldn't focus on anything at all.

"Come on, I don't have all day," the man growled, seemingly unaware that Remington couldn't hear him. "For the last time: How did you find us?" He drew his gun and pointed it Remington, but everything was still too blurry, and the man's voice just sounded like background noise.

"WE HAVE TO HURRY!" Scott said. "Go faster!"

"Scott, please," McKinley said. "Calm down. I'm going as fast as I can without risking an accident."

The GPS was telling them that they still had another 5 minutes to go. But Scott worried that 5 minutes would be too long. Sure, he had just met Remington, and even though it wasn't his fault, he knew he would feel responsible if Remington died because she was trying to save him.

McKinley turned the car off the main road and onto a series of small, single lane roads.

"How many abandoned buildings that I didn't know about are there in this town?" Scott asked, curiously.

"A lot," McKinley said, struggling to keep the car on the small, winding road. The GPS said that the location of the car was about 2 minutes away, and Scott was holding his breath the entire time.

Finally, the car came into view and Scott was the first to point it out. "There!" he shouted.

McKinley shut the car off and looked around. There was a small house, covered in weeds and vines a few yards away from the car. McKinley drew his gun cautiously and he walked over to the house.

THE MAN STILL DIDN'T seem to notice that Remington could see him or hear anything that he was saying. Instead, he thought that she was ignoring him.

"Forget it!" he said. "If you're not going to tell me, I'll find out myself." He pulled the trigger on the gun and aimed for Remington's head.

"Police, freeze!" McKinley shouted, kicking the rotting door down and aiming his gun at the man.

Cursing, the man dove through a shattered window out to the back of the house and took off running. McKinley fired his gun at the man, but the bullet sailed over his head, and into the woods behind the house.

Scott ran into the building behind McKinley and rushed over to Remington as McKinley tried to follow the thief through the woods.

"Remington!" Scott said, untying her ropes. "What happened?"

"Scott..." Remington said softly. Scott noticed the knife in her arm and shouted for McKinley.

"She needs to get to a hospital!" Scott said. "Look at her arm."

Remington was barely conscious now and eyelids were fluttering. McKinley holstered his gun, lifted Remington up off the chair and carried her into the car outside.

"The hospital isn't that far from here," McKinley said. "No sense waiting for an ambulance." He started the engine, and peeled away from the house.

"What happened to the thief?" Scott asked.

"He got away," McKinley said. "He disappeared somewhere in the woods. How's Remington doing?"

"Not good," Scott said. Remington was no longer conscious, but Scott could feel her heart still beating, although faintly. "How far are we from the hospital?"

"Almost there," McKinley said, speeding the car up. They got to the hospital in maybe 2 minutes and McKinley pulled the car right up to the front. He carried Remington into the hospital where one of the nurses laid her on a stretcher and brought her to a hospital room.

"Does she have parents or someone that we should call?" McKinley asked Scott.

"I don't think her parents would even care," Scott said. "Plus, I don't even know how we'd get into contact with them."

McKinley nodded. "She'll be alright here," he said. "Do you need a doctor to check you out and make sure you're okay?"

Scott shook his head. "I'm fine," he said. "Just a couple of cuts and bruises."

"If you're sure," McKinley said. "We need to get you home now, though. Don't worry, I'll keep you updated on Remington's status."

"Before you take me home, can we get my stuff back?" Scott asked. "From the warehouse where I was taken first."

"Do you remember where the warehouse was?" McKinley asked Scott.

Scott shook his head again. "No, I think I was unconscious on the ride there." He rubbed the back of his head. "That's probably going to be a bruise."

"Are you sure you don't want a doctor?" McKinley asked.

"Really, I'm fine," Scott said. "I don't remember how I got to the warehouse, but I think it was the same place that they brought Erica to last time."

"How can you be sure?" McKinley asked.

"I can't," said Scott. "But it looked familiar to me, so I'm guessing it's the same place."

"Okay, I guess it can't hurt," McKinley said. "I just got a text from Officer Miles. They've finished processing the other thief, but he claims he has no idea where his partner might have gone."

Scott followed McKinley back out to his car and said, "You know, they told me that this was 'a lot deeper than I realized' when they kidnapped me."

"What did they mean by that?" McKinley asked, as he pulled the car out of the hospital and onto the main road.

Scott shrugged. "I don't know. I thought maybe he was bluffing, but I don't think that someone would go through all this trouble just to steal a couple-thousand dollars in things."

"You're right," McKinley said. "There's probably more to this then meets the eye. And I'm willing to be that his partner knows what's going on."

"I thought he's not willing to talk, though," Scott said.

"He's not," McKinley replied. "And if he truly is an ex-police officer like our original suspicions were, he's not going to talk either."

"So, what do we do?" Scott asked.

"For you," McKinley said. "Same thing as I told you before. Nothing. The same goes for Remington. And Phoebe."

"But what if they come after me again?" Scott asked. "You told me to avoid walking places by myself and I did that. They still came after me."

"I've decided to assign Officer Harris to watch you when you're not in school," McKinley replied. "But he's the only officer I could spare."

McKinley pulled the car up to the abandoned warehouse where the thieves had brought Erica to a couple of weeks prior. "This is the place."

Scott climbed out of the car and started towards the door when McKinley raised his hand and said, "Wait. Let me go in first."

Keeping his hand on his holster, McKinley cautiously walked into the warehouse and looked around. The place was empty as far as eye could see, but the smell of smoke still lingered in the air.

Scott waved his hand in front of his face to clear some of the smoke. "This must be the place," he said. "That has to be from the smoke bomb that Remington threw."

Scott and McKinley walked into the building and looked around for Scott's belongings.

"Found 'em!" Scott said. He was standing next to a support pillar and his bag was leaning up against it. The bag had been gone through, but nothing seemed to be missing.

Impressively, Scott's laptop and phone were still there, undamaged, but a bit smoky. Scott checked his phone and saw a bunch of missed texts, all from Phoebe, Adrian, and Erica.

"Scott, you can read your texts later," McKinley said. "Now that we've gotten your stuff back, let's get you home."

Scott nodded, and shoved his phone into his pocket. He stuffed everything back into his backpack, picked it up, and headed back outside with McKinley.

Chapter VI

6:30 PM. Adrian's family and Erica had finally arrived at the campsite after the long eight-hour drive. Adrian's dad pulled the RV over to their registered spot and leaned back in his chair.

"What a relief!" he said. "You can only drive for so long before you start to get exhausted."

Adrian laughed. "At least we didn't get any more flat tires."

"I think I would have just gone home if we got another flat tire," Adrian's dad said, getting out of the driver's seat. "Can you two help me hook the RV up?"

"I've never done that before," Erica said. "I don't really know what to do."

"It's easy," Adrian said. "Here, I'll show you."

They climbed out of the RV and Adrian led Erica around the other side where the electrical and water hook-ups were. He was demonstrating how to hook up the water line when Erica's phone started to vibrate.

"It's Phoebe," Erica said, pulling her phone out of her pocket. "I told her we'd probably get to the campsite around 6-7."

Erica answered the video call and Phoebe's face popped up on the screen.

"Erica! Hi!" Phoebe said. "Did you guys get to the campsite yet?"

"Yep, just a few minutes ago," Erica said. "We're just setting up the RV now."

"How was the trip?" Phoebe asked.

"It was long...and a bit disastrous," Adrian said, joining the call. "But other than that, it was fun."

"Disastrous?" Phoebe asked, a little confused. "What happened?"

"We got stranded with a flat tire in the middle of nowhere," Erica said. "I didn't get a chance to tell you over texts, so I figured I'd tell you when you called."

"Yikes," Phoebe said. "But at least you made it."

"Yep," Adrian said. "A few hours late, but other than that, we made it."

"Say, where's Scott?" Erica asked. "Isn't he going to join the call?"

Phoebe shrugged. "I don't know. He left school with some girl named Remington and I haven't heard from him since."

"Remington? Whose Remington?" Adrian asked.

"Long story," Phoebe said. "But the slimmed down version is basically this: Remington stole Scott's wallet, so Scott said that his parents might be able to get her a job at their store so she can stop stealing. He was going to take her to the store after school."

"I feel like you left out a lot of details," Adrian said, scratching his head. "School ended about 4 hours ago. Where is he now?"

"I don't know, okay," Phoebe said, frustrated. "Why do you care?"

"Woah, geez," Erica said. "Is something going on?"

"No," Phoebe said. "Why would there be?"

"I don't know," Erica said. "You just seem more...agitated than usual."

"It's just that I think Scott's making a mistake, offering Remington a job at his parent's store," Phoebe said. "She is a thief, you know."

"Well, I don't know Remington, since I've never met her, but it sounds like Scott's just trying to do a nice thing," Adrian said.

"Yeah, but what if doing that nice thing put his parents in danger?" Phoebe asked.

"Phoebe, she's a 14-year-old girl, not a mass murderer," Erica broke in. "She's the same age as you. Honestly, I think you're just overreacting."

"That's exactly what Scott said," Phoebe replied. "But what if she steals something from their store?"

"Phoebe, be reasonable," Adrian said. "Their store has security cameras, and I don't think she's a professional thief. If she steals something, Scott tells Officer McKinley or Miles and they go talk to her."

Phoebe sighed. "I guess you're right. I should talk to Scott and apologize."

"You should talk to Remington as well," Erica said. "Maybe if you got to know her better, you'd think of her differently."

Phoebe nodded. "Alright, I'll talk to Scott and Remington later. In the meantime, how's the campsite?"

"It's beautiful," Erica said. "The weather is perfect, and it almost reminds me of the nature preserve back in North Carolina."

"Sounds nice," Phoebe said. "Do you guys have anything planned for tonight?"

Adrian shook his head. "Nope, tonight we're probably going to just set the RV up and maybe explore the campground a little."

"Anything interesting happening back in North Carolina?" Erica asked.

Phoebe deliberated a little bit, unsure whether to tell Erica about the thieves escaping or not. She decided not to, since she didn't want to spoil their vacation.

"Nope, not really," Phoebe said. "Other than Scott and Remington, pretty much everything is the same."

"Sounds exciting," Adrian said. He looked over his shoulder and saw his Dad waving at them to come over and help. "Well, my Dad needs me to help him out with something, so I'll talk to you guys later!"

"Have fun in Michigan!" Phoebe said, before waving goodbye and leaving the call.

After hanging up, Phoebe decided to tell Adrian what was going on. She texted Adrian, and let him know about the thieves escaping. But she told him not to tell Erica, as to not ruin her vacation.

Phoebe put the phone down and thought for a while. Finally, she made up her mind and decided that Adrian was right about what he had said about Remington and Scott.

Phoebe grabbed her phone and keys and headed out to talk to Scott and apologize. She came to Scott's house shortly after McKinley had dropped Scott off.

Phoebe knocked on the door and Scott opened the door.

"Hey Phoebe, I was just about to call you." Scott said.

Phoebe raised her eyebrows. "What happened to you?" she asked, noticing Scott's decidedly unkempt appearance, the bruise on his face, and the cut under his eye.

"Long story," Scott said. "Here, come on in." He gestured to the front door and Phoebe stepped inside.

"You're a mess," Phoebe said. "And how did it go with Remington?"

Scott took a seat on the couch and said, "Alright, let me explain." Phoebe took a seat on a chair across from Scott and Scott told Phoebe the story of what had happened to them and Remington.

Phoebe rubbed her forehead. "I'm so confused," she said. "So, the thieves attacked you and Remington after school, when you two were walking to your parents' store?"

"That's right," Scott said. "They took me and ignored Remington. But Remington was able to toss a tracker onto their car and figure out where they took me."

"Where did she get a tracker from?" Phoebe asked.

Scott shrugged. "There's a lot of things that I don't know about her."

"So, how is she now?" Phoebe asked.

"Officer McKinley took her to the hospital," Scott replied. "She was in pretty bad shape when we found her, though."

"Is she going to be alright?" Phoebe asked, concerned.

Scott bit his lip. "I don't know," he said. "Officer McKinley said that he would call me if he got any news from the hospital, but I haven't heard anything from her yet."

"Do her parents know?" Phoebe asked. "I feel like someone should tell her."

Scott shook his head. "Nobody even knows how to get in contact with them," he said. "And judging from what Remington told me about them, I don't know if they'd even care."

Phoebe shook her head. "That's not right. She might've died, and her parents don't even know or probably care. If it was me, my parents would be at the hospital the entire time."

"I know," Scott said. "It's like Remington said. Not everybody's life is picture-perfect."

"Maybe not picture-perfect, but that's on another level," Phoebe said. "There has to be something that we can do."

"Like what?" Scott asked. "And besides, I thought you didn't even trust her. You told me not to offer her a job at my parents' store."

Phoebe sighed. "I know, and I'm sorry," she said. "I just don't trust people that easily. But she might have saved your life. If she pulls through this, the very least we can do if get her a job."

Scott nodded. "Have you heard from Adrian and Erica?" he asked.

"Yeah, they called a few minutes ago," Phoebe said. "They got to the campsite, but they got a flat tire on the way there, so they arrived late."

"Well, it happens to everybody eventually," Scott said. Suddenly, Scott's phone rang, making him jump.

"It's Officer McKinley," Scott said, picking it up.

"Scott, the hospital gave me a call," McKinley said. "Remington's awake."

"Thanks!" Scott said. "I'll go pay her a visit." Scott hung up the phone and told Phoebe what McKinley had said.

"How far is the hospital from here?" Phoebe asked.

"It's about a 20-minute walk," Scott said, grabbing his keys. "You want to come with me?"

"Of course!" Phoebe said, getting up off the couch and following Scott outside. They walked to the hospital and got there at around 7pm.

"Hi, do you know what room Remington is in?" Scott asked the receptionist at the front desk.

"Last name?" the receptionist asked.

"Uhhh, I'm not actually sure," Scott said. "I don't think she ever told me. How many Remington's can there be at this hospital anyway?"

"One second," the receptionist said, checking her computer. "Just one. Remington Cassidy. 14."

"That's her," Scott said. "What room is she in?"

"Your name first," the receptionist said. "And yours as well." She gestured to Phoebe.

"Scott Curtis," Scott replied.

"And Phoebe Mason," Phoebe said.

"Perfect," the receptionist entering something in the computer. She slid a pad over to Scott and Phoebe. "Just sign here please."

Phoebe and Scott both put their signature on the pad and the receptionist said, "Room 232. Second floor."

Scott thanked the receptionist, and Scott and Phoebe headed for the elevator. They took it up to the second floor like the receptionist had directed them to and Scott found Room 232.

Phoebe knocked on the door, and Remington said, "Come in." She was lying on the hospital bed. Her arm and head were both bandaged, and she looked paler than usual, but other than that, she seemed okay.

"We thought we'd drop by to see you," Scott said. "How are you doing?"

Remington shrugged. "Better," she said. "They gave me a blood transfusion, and some pain killers, but my arm still hurts."

"Scott told me what happened," Phoebe said.

"Yeah, one minute I was pointing a shotgun at them, and the next minute I have a knife in my arm and I'm being tackled," Remington said. "These guys must be trained fighters or something."

"What exactly happened after I left you to go call Officer McKinley?" Scott asked. "If you don't mind my asking," he quickly added.

"No, it's fine," Remington said, sitting up a little. "Like I said, I was pointing a shotgun at them, and then my head started to hurt. I guess it must have distracted me, because the guy who I didn't shoot threw a knife at my arm.

I don't know what happened after that, though. I remember getting really dizzy and weak, and I think I might have collapsed. Then I remember waking up in some abandoned house or something."

"That's where we found you," Scott said. "In an abandoned and falling apart house off of Route 34."

"Yeah," Remington said. "I remember the guy asked me how much I knew. I told him I didn't know anything, but he didn't believe me, so he tortured me." Remington winced, remembering how the thief had twisted the knife in her arm. "I told him I only knew what Scott had told me. That they were thieves who kidnapped your friend and made her break into houses for them. He finally believed me, but he wanted to know how I found them after they kidnapped Scott.

I don't remember if I told them or not, though. I remember kicking him in the stomach, but I don't remember much after that until I woke up here." Remington leaned back on the bed and rested her arm the bedside.

"I'm sorry you got involved," Scott said. "I never thought that they would be so desperate to find Erica."

"It's not your fault," Remington said. "But the guy said something about robbing the first two houses only being a test. And that the real challenge was yet to come."

"What did he mean by that?" Phoebe asked. "The real challenge?"

Remington shrugged. "No idea. Did they catch the guy?" she asked.

"One of them," Scott said. "They one who threw the knife at you left behind his partner and the police arrested him."

"What about the other one?" Remington asked.

"He escaped into the woods, somewhere," Scott said. "He dove through a window after McKinley stormed the place."

Remington sighed. "Of course he did. You think he'll come after me again?"

"I don't know," Scott said. "I wouldn't have thought that they would come after me, but they did anyway. And we all thought that once they escaped prison, they would try and leave the country, but they didn't. So, everything we've thought about these criminals has been wrong."

"Whatever they're planning must be really big," Phoebe said. "You should let Officer McKinley know what they told you."

"Yeah, you're right," Remington said. "How do I get in contact in him?"

"You could always just tell me," a voice said from behind them. Scott whirled around and saw Officer Miles standing near the doorway.

"Officer Miles!" Remington exclaimed. "What are you doing here?"

"Wait, you two know each other?" Phoebe asked. "You've never met."

"Oh, we've met before," Officer Miles said. "I'll tell you how later." To Remington, she said, "McKinley told me what happened. I decided to check up on you and see how you are doing."

"Like I told Scott, better," Remington said. "I'm not in trouble or anything, am I?"

"Trouble? No, of course not," Officer Miles said. "What you did might have been foolish, but it certainly was heroic."

Miles turned to Scott and Phoebe. "Is it okay if you two clear the room for a bit. I'd like to talk to Remington alone."

Scott and Phoebe nodded and both left the hospital room, leaving Miles and Remington alone.

"So, Remington," Miles started. "Have you been on the straight and narrow?"

"I suppose..." Remington said.

"You suppose?" Miles asked. "It's a yes or no question."

"Well, I tried," Remington said. "But what am I supposed to do? Not eat?"

"I told you," Miles said. "If you need help, you can always come to me. I'd be happy to help you out."

"I know, I know," Remington said. "But that's not really in my nature. I don't like asking for help. I'd rather do things on my own."

"Sure, and I get it," Miles said. "But asking for help is better than stealing. Look, I'm proud of what you did for Scott, but remember what I told. Once you turn 16, I can't help you out anymore." She patted Remington on the shoulder. "I'll leave you to rest. We can talk about you staying out of trouble later."

Remington waved goodbye to Miles as she left the room. Outside, Scott and Phoebe were sitting on waiting chairs in the hallway. They both stood up when Miles came outside.

"Officer Miles, how *do* you know Remington?" Phoebe asked.

"Remington has a record," Miles said. "Once she got her third strike on her record, for auto theft, she would have been sent to juvenile hall for a few years. She's a bright girl, though. Being sent to juvenile hall would take away any future she might have. So, as the arresting officer, I convinced the judges to let her off, with the promise that I would keep tabs on her and make sure she didn't get on the wrong side of the law again."

"Is that why she didn't want to go to the police after I was kidnapped?" Scott asked.

"Probably," Officer Miles said. "That, and Remington has always been the kind of person to do things her on own. It comes from constantly having to fend for herself and her parents never being there for her."

"Remington told me about her parents," Scott said. "Isn't there anything that we can do to help her?"

Miles shook her head. "Not really. Remington is a teenager, so I can't really have child services come take her away. Nobody really adopts teenagers, so she'd just be bounced around foster homes until she turned 18, and that would only make things worse."

"But her parents-" Scott started. Miles held up her hand. "Scott, I know. But it's not your concern. I appreciate your wanting to help, and I'm sure Remington does as well, but this has nothing to do with you."

"I was thinking that my parents could hire her to work at their store," Scott said. "That's actually where we were going when we got ambushed."

"That's a really good idea, Scott," Miles said. "I can talk to your parents and see if they'd be open to hiring Remington. Of course, they'd need to know about her record, but I think it's worth a shot."

"Officer Miles," Phoebe broke in. "Remington said that the thieves told her the two houses that they made Erica rob were just a test and that the real challenge was coming."

Miles bit her lip. "That does not sound good." She grabbed her car keys and said "You two should get home now, while I get back to the police station to let Officer McKinley know."

Scott and Phoebe poked their head into Remington's room and said goodbye before they left. They said goodbye to Officer Miles and then each headed home.

REMINGTON LAY AWAKE in her hospital bed, thinking about what Officer Miles had said and about what had happened to her. She was pondering everything when she heard someone say, "Hi!" from the room over.

Curious, Remington pushed the curtain aside, and saw a little girl lying on a bed in the room next to her. She had dark brown, curly hair, and light brown eyes, which contrasted with her hair color perfectly.

The girl waved to Remington and said, "I'm Josephine. What's your name?"

"I'm Remington," Remington replied. "What are you here for?"

"Broken arm," Josephine responded, showing Remington the cast on her arm. "What about you?"

"Uhh, it's a long story," Remington said, not entirely sure what to tell her.

Josephine laughed. "There's not much else to do except talk to each other," she said.

"Well, let's just say that I had a run-in with some people who weren't as friendly as they could be," Remington responded.

"That's it?" Josephine. "That's all you're going to tell me?"

"Well, there's more to it, but I don't think that you'd believe me if I told you," Remington responded.

"Well, even if I don't believe you, I like stories," Josephine said. She pointed to the stack of books on the table next to her. "The nurse brought these over when I said I was bored."

"Alright, well, get comfortable," Remington said. "Like I said, it's a long story."

"I'm as comfortable as I can be," Josephine responded, propping herself up on a pillow.

"Okay, so it all started when...." Remington told Josephine the story of what had happened to her, trying to avoid all the rather gruesome details, but still giving her the main gist.

"That's fascinating!" Josephine said, after Remington had finished telling her story. "You should write a book about your adventures. I'd read it!"

"Well, I'm not really much of a writer," Remington said. "Do you like to write?"

"Me?" Josephine asked. "A little, I guess. I like drawing more than writing, actually."

"What do you draw?" Remington asked.

"All kinds of things," Josephine said. "Here, I'll show you." She reached down and grabbed a piece of paper from the floor and showed it to Remington. It was a drawing of a guinea pig in a cage. Remington was impressed with the amount of detail and dedication put into the drawing.

"This is really good!" she told Josephine. "It's really detailed and well-drawn."

Josephine smiled. "Thanks!" she said. "It's a drawing of my pet guinea pig. She's back at home."

"How old are you?" Remington asked, curious now.

"11," Josephine said. "Most people tell me I look young for my age."

"They're not wrong," Remington said. "I thought you were about 8 or 9. Where are your parents?" Remington had realized that she hadn't seen any sign of Josephine's parents.

Josephine shrugged. "They're not around much. And when they are around, they just fight with each other."

Remington nodded. "I know what that's like," she said. "Do you go to school?"

"Of course," Josephine said. "My parents don't have a car, though. So, I have to walk to school every day."

"What about food?" Remington asked. "How do you pay for school lunches?"

"I don't," Josephine said. "There's a man who owns a restaurant that's on the way to school. He gives me a free meal to take to school every day."

Remington smiled. "That's nice of him." She was starting to see a lot of similarities between her and Josephine. It was almost as Josephine was the younger sister that she never had.

"So, what do you do after school?" Remington asked.

"Homework," Josephine said. "And I draw. And sometimes I play with Nibbles. That's the name of my guinea pig."

"Do your parents know that you're here?" Remington asked. "Did the doctors tell them?"

"They're actually my foster parents," Josephine said. "I've never met my real parents, but I think the doctors called my parents."

"You're an orphan?" Remington asked.

Josephine nodded. "The orphanage doesn't know who my real parents are. According to them, I was found on the front step of the building, but there was no information about who I was. I've lived with a bunch of different foster families, but I try to not let that bother me."

"Do you have any siblings?" Remington asked. "Sisters? Brothers?"

Josephine shook her head. "I don't think so, but some of the families that I've stayed with had other kids. I never really got along with any of them, though."

"Do your foster parents not treat you well?" Remington asked. "You said they aren't home much and you have to get meals from the man who owns the restaurant."

"Well, they give me a place to live," Josephine said. "And I have my own room. But other than that, they don't really care much about me."

Remington thought back to when she was 11. Sure, she wasn't an orphan, but her parents had treated her the same way Josephine's parents had treated Josephine. They gave her a place to sleep, but not much after that.

Remington had spent most of her time learning skills like pickpocketing, lock-picking, and hot-wiring. Skills that she knew she would find useful, since she spent most her time on the streets, but she had never really developed any actual hobbies the way Josephine had.

Josephine and Remington talked for another hour, becoming friends in the process. Remington learned the Josephine's life had been a lot similar to hers' but she had managed to get though it without needed to steal or pickpocket.

Eventually, Josephine said that she was getting tired. Remington realized that it was almost 11pm, and that the two of them had been talking for almost 3 hours. Josephine had been right: There really wasn't much else to do except talk to each other.

They said good night to each other, and Remington pulled the curtain back. She stayed awake for a while, thinking about the conversation that she had with Josephine for a while, before finally falling asleep.

Chapter VII

I t was the next morning. Officer Miles was sitting across from the thief whom Remington had shot in the leg, trying to gain any information about the whereabouts of his partner or their master plan.

"I know you know where your partner is," Miles said. "Right now we have you on kidnapping, robbery, and I'm sure I can throw on a few others to your sentence. If you don't tell me where your partner is, you're going to take the fall for all of it."

The man stared at Miles with a stony look on his face. His leg had been bandaged, and he was sitting next to the lawyer that had been provided to him by the state.

"I have no idea who you're talking about," he said simply. "I have no partner."

Miles leaned forward and said, "Trust me, you don't want to play this game with me. Now, where is your partner?"

The man shrugged. "Who?" he asked.

Miles' face turned cold. "Your partner kidnapped and tortured a teenage girl," she said. "If my partner hadn't found her in time, he would have killed her as well. So, tell me, what plan could you possibly have that you would go to such measures to fulfill?"

"Plan?" the man asked. "What plan are you talking about?"

"Face the facts," Miles said. "If we don't find your partner, you're going away for conspiracy to commit murder as well as all your other crimes. So, are you going to help us or not?"

The man smirked. "I see no benefit in helping you. Now, if you have anymore questions, please ask them to this crummy lawyer that the state gave me." The man leaned back in his chair and closed his eyes.

Miles stormed out of the room as Officer Wesley brought the man back to his cell. Miles walked back to her desk and slammed her fist on the table. "We're getting nowhere with him," she said to McKinley.

"Officer Harris and Wesley already searched the car that the thief left behind," McKinley said. "There was nothing to be found in there, and as expected, the car was stolen anyway."

"We don't even know their names," Miles said. "They had no ID on them, and they refused to tell us when we arrested them. All we have is their DNA and fingerprints."

"I searched through all the criminal databases," McKinley said. "Their fingerprints and DNA weren't in any of them."

"Wait a minute," Miles said. "Remember how we first thought they were ex-cops?"

"Yes..." McKinley said. "But police stations don't keep records of DNA and fingerprints of all their officers."

"Sure, but what about headshots?" Miles asked. "Their photo must be somewhere."

"Of course!" McKinley said, pulling up the criminals' mugshots. "I'll run them through all the databases of current or former police officers."

The scan went for about 5 minutes, before a hit finally came up on one of them.

"Wait, look at this," McKinley said, pointing to the screen. "One of them served as an officer in the Raleigh Police Department for 5 years."

"Which one?" Miles asked, leaning over to look at McKinley's screen.

"The one who escaped," McKinley said. "There's no record of his partner anywhere, but the one who escaped is named Steven Rockwood."

"Hold on, look at this," Miles said. "It says that he quit the police force shortly after his wife, Oliva Rockwood, was murdered."

"And they never figured out who did it," McKinley said. "You don't think…"

"Maybe, but that doesn't explain anything," Miles said. "If he did murder his wife, why would he be robbing houses. And what did he need Erica for?"

"There's obviously a piece of the puzzle we're missing," McKinley said. "Unless…"

"Unless what?" Miles asked.

"Well, this might be crazy, but what if he didn't do it," McKinley said. "What if he decided to take justice into his own hands and hunt down the actual killer."

Miles squinted. "No, that doesn't fit his personality at all," she said. "If he truly was acting like a vigilante, he wouldn't have kidnapped Erica, or anybody else for that matter. There's something else going on here."

"According to Remington, Rockwood said that the real challenge was yet to come," McKinley said. "And that the first two robberies were just a test."

"What are you thinking?" Miles asked.

"Well, what if he just wanted to test Erica's skills?" McKinley said. "And once he was sure Erica was ready, they would go ahead with what he referred to as "The Challenge"."

"But what is the challenge?" Miles asked. "It obviously has to be something important. Why else would he go through all this trouble?"

"I don't know…" McKinley said. "Officer Wesley!"

Officer Wesley stuck his head into the office. "Yeah chief?"

"I need all the files and information on the Rockwood case," McKinley said. "Give me everything you can find."

"On it," Wesley said, heading back to his desk.

"I'm guessing that there's a connection between that case and his activity now," McKinley said. "We just need to find it."

"REMINGTON, ARE YOU sure you're okay to go back to school so soon?" Scott was surprised to see Remington in school the next morning, expecting her to still be in the hospital.

"The doctor said that I could stay another day if I felt like I needed to, but I should be okay to return home," Remington said.

"You know, I never really got to thank you for saving my life," Scott said. "If you hadn't showed up at the warehouse when you did, I might not be here right now."

"Well, it's what friends do, I suppose," Remington said. "You offered me a job, so I saved your life. Sounds even enough."

Scott laughed and asked. "Do you still want that job?"

"Of course!" Remington said. "We can redo our conversation that we were having yesterday, and hopefully not get ambushed this time."

The bell rang so Scott and Remington dashed off to class. Scott ran into Phoebe on his way to the first class, but since there wasn't much time to talk, they each gave each other a quick hello before heading off to their first class.

During lunch period, Scott got his food and took a seat at the groups' usual table. Phoebe was still in line, so Scott looked around the room. He noticed that Remington was sitting at a table in the far corner of the room, alone.

Scott walked over to Remington and said, "Hey, why don't you come join me and Phoebe?"

"Oh, thanks!" Remington said. "I'm just so used to sitting by myself." She grabbed her food tray and followed Scott to the table where he was sitting. Phoebe joined them a bit later and Scott asked, "So, what do you think is going on?"

"What do you mean?" Phoebe asked. "We're eating lunch at school."

"No, not us," Scott said. "The thieves. What's the "real challenge" and why is it so important."

Remington shrugged. "I dunno. But they're pretty desperate to get whatever it is done. I told everything that I knew to Officer Miles, so I'm sure they must have a lead by now."

Scott was about to say something when Remington suddenly stood up and called, "Josephine!"

The school that the students went to was rather strange in some respects. The high school and middle school buildings were right next to each other, and even though the high school and middle school classes were held in different buildings, lunch period was held in the high school cafeteria for both middle-schoolers and high-schoolers. According to the principal, this was done to save money, since they would have to hire less chefs, and it would be easier to organize everything.

Josephine, who was holding her lunch tray, turned to see Remington. She waved and walked over to sit with Remington.

"Scott, Phoebe, this is Josephine," Remington said. "I met her at the hospital yesterday."

"Hi!" Josephine said. "Remington told me about you guys. You're Phoebe." She pointed to Phoebe. "And you're Scott."

"That's us, alright!" Scott said. He gestured to the empty seat across from Remington and invited her to sit down. Josephine put her lunch tray down and took a seat.

"How old are you?" Phoebe asked.

Josephine laughed. "Everybody asks me that. I'm 11."

"How exactly did you two meet?" Scott asked.

"Oh, Josephine was in the room next to mine," Remington said. "She had a broken arm."

"Well, I gathered as much," Scott said, looking at Josephine's cast. "Mind if I sign it?"

"Of course not!" Josephine said, holding out her arm. Scott grabbed a pen from his bag, and signed his name on Josephine's cast. Phoebe followed suit and then so did Remington.

"You know, Remington told me a fantastic story yesterday," Josephine said. "You should tell it to them too."

"I think they already know," Remington said, chuckling.

"You do?" Josephine asked. "Did she tell you already?"

"What story is it?" Phoebe asked.

"How she got the cut on her arm," Josephine said. "It was a great story. I said that she should write a book about it. She'd be a great storywriter."

"Well, it just so happens that the story she told you is true," Scott said. "Although, it does sound made up."

"Wait, really?" Josephine said. "That actually happened?"

"I did say so," Remington said, laughing. "You just didn't believe me."

"It just sounded made-up," Josephine said. Her dark eyes twinkled. "So, are you guys detectives?"

Now Phoebe laughed. "No, just teenagers. Who somehow got involved in something very dangerous. Something that you don't want to get involved in as well."

"If you say so," Josephine said. "But it sounds fascinating!" She reached down in her backpack and pulled out a piece of paper. "Phoebe, Remington said that you looked like the kind of person who likes drawing. Is that true?"

"Um, well, sometimes," Phoebe said. "I'm not very good at it, but I do it to clear my mind sometimes."

Josephine handed the piece of paper to Phoebe and asked, "What do you think of this drawing?"

Phoebe unrolled the piece of paper to reveal a drawing of a pink unicorn with a rainbow horn. It was drawn with watercolor crayons, and, the same way Remington had been with the drawing of the Guinea Pig, Phoebe was impressed with the amount of detail.

"This is impressive!" Phoebe said. "Did you draw this?"

Josephine nodded. "Is it really that good?" she asked. "Aside from you and Remington, nobody's ever told me that it was great before."

"Trust me," Phoebe said. "For someone your age, this tops the charts." She was about to say more, but the lunch bell rang. "Time to head back to class," Phoebe said. "But, like I said, your artistry is impressive!"

MCKINLEY WAS DIGGING through piles of paperwork, gathering all the information he could on the Rockwood case, when Officer Wesley knocked on the door.

"Chief, you've got to see this," he said.

McKinley looked up from the stack of papers and grabbed a bunch. "Okay, just a second." He followed Wesley to his desk, and Miles joined him there.

"What's going on?" Miles asked.

"Okay, so I was looking through all the old case files, regarding Rockwood's murder, right," Wesley said. "And this jumped out at me." He pointed to a file on the screen.

"So, it turns out that Mrs. Rockwood had recently taken out a $5,000,000 life insurance policy on herself. In fact, she took it out just days before she was killed," Wesley said.

"Wait, *she* took it out?" Miles asked. "Was the beneficiary the husband?"

"No, and that's the odd part," Wesley said. "Steven Rockwood wouldn't get any of the money. The money would all go to the Rockwood's daughter, Victoria Rockwood."

"And where is Victoria Rockwood now?" McKinley asked.

"Well, as far as we're concerned, she doesn't exist," Wesley said.

"I'm sorry, what?" Miles asked. "She doesn't exist?"

"There was no evidence of any daughter in the Rockwood's house," Wesley answered. "And Steven Rockwood denied any knowledge of his wife ever being pregnant or having a daughter."

"That doesn't make sense," Miles said. "How could she name the beneficiary of a life insurance policy as someone who doesn't exist. Did they check with hospital records?"

"Yep," Wesley nodded. "No hospitals report anyone that matched Olivia Rockwood's description ever having a baby there, and her name isn't in any hospital report."

"It could have been a home birth," McKinley suggested. "But why wouldn't Steven Rockwood have known about it?"

"What if he did?" Miles said. "And he lied about it so he could collect the life insurance instead."

"Now here's where it gets really, really weird," Wesley said, pulling up another page of the report. "Look here. As it turns out, Steven Rockwood did attempt to claim the life insurance, saying that the beneficiary didn't exist. But the insurance company claimed that the child did exist, and that a trust had been set up for the child. The money was to be given to Victoria when she turned 18."

"What about Steven?" Miles asked. "And how did the insurance company know that Victoria existed?"

"Olivia specifically said that Steven was not to be granted access to the trust," Wesley responded. "And when questioned by the police, the insurance agent claimed that Olivia had sent proof of Victoria's existence."

"What proof?" McKinley asked.

"He wouldn't say," Wesley said. "And without a warrant, they couldn't force him to give up the information."

"Here's a thought," McKinley said. "What if Steven Rockwood found out where Victoria Rockwood was, and in order to get access to the trust fund, he's trying to get to her."

"That makes sense, actually," Wesley said, flipping though one of the case files. "In order for Rockwood to gain access to the trust, Victoria would need to sign a waiver, and both of them needed to be present, along with a witness."

"How old would Victoria be?" Miles asked. "Doesn't she have to be at least 18 for her to give access to the trust?"

"Olivia claimed that Victoria was less than a year old when she set up the insurance policy," Wesley said. "This was about 10 years ago, so she would be around 10 or 11 now."

"Okay, that makes no sense," Miles said. "Like I said, doesn't she have to be 18 before she can sign anything legally binding?"

"Normally, yes," Wesley said. "But in this case, since her father, Steven, claimed that she didn't exist, and claimed no responsibility for her, the only person who could sign was her, since she had no legal guardian. A DNA test would have to be done, to prove that it was indeed Victoria Rockwood signing, but after that, she was free to sign the trust off to whomever she wanted."

"Were there no relatives or anything?" McKinley asked.

"According to the report, Olivia was an only child, and her parents died before Victoria was born. And Steven's parents were also dead. He has a brother, but he's currently in a mental asylum, so there was no way he was taking custody of Victoria," Wesley said.

"But nobody even knows where Victoria is?" Miles asked. "Or if she even exists."

"Aside from the insurance agent, who supposedly had proof of her existence, there's nothing about her," Wesley said.

"Had proof?" Miles asked.

"He died of a heart attack last year," Wesley said. "His wife burned all his papers and documents and wiped all his computers."

"Why on earth for?" McKinley asked.

"She claimed that she was concerned that her husband was involved in shady activities, and she didn't want something to tarnish his memory," Wesley responded. "And the agent cleared every last bit of information about Victoria Rockwood out of the insurance company before he died."

"Wouldn't that make the insurance policy null and void?" Miles asked. "If all the information about her was destroyed?"

"No, not really," McKinley broke in. "Since the money was already paid out, there was no way to void the contract."

Miles shook her head. "This is ridiculous. We have a potential murderer on the loose, possibly hunting for a child that we don't even know exists or not."

"Hey, chief." An officer poked his head into Wesley's office. "We found something in the perp's car. It was stashed in his glove compartment."

Miles, McKinley, and Wesley followed Officer Winston to the evidence room, where Winston showed the three of them a piece of paper with: NCSB, SDB 198 written on it.

"What does that mean?" Miles asked.

"Not sure," Winston responded. "I've been running down possible meanings, but nothing jumps out."

"NCSB. National Cybersecurity and Biotechnology, National College of Sports Medicine Board, there's a whole bunch of things that could stand for," McKinley said.

"NC could be North Carolina," Miles said. "That would make sense. North Carolina State Bar, North Carolina State…"

"No, not State Bar," McKinley interrupted. "North Carolina State Bank."

"Okay, that fits," Miles said. "What about SDB?"

"State Depository Branch, Security and Data Division," McKinley suggested. "Wait no. What about "Safety Deposit Box?""

"North Carolina State Bank, Safety Deposit Box 198," Miles said. "That makes perfect sense." Who owns that box?"

"Uhh, it's registered to an "Olive Stonewood," Winston said, checking the database.

Miles and McKinley looked at each other. "Olive Stonewood?" Miles asked.

Winston double-checked. "Yep, that's correct. Why?"

"Olivia Rockwood," McKinley said. "That's the name of Steven Rockwood's wife. Olive Stonewood seems awfully similar to Oliva Rockwood."

"Agreed," Miles said. "We need to figure out what's in the safety deposit box before Steven gets to it."

ERICA WAS SITTING ON top of the RV with Adrian, enjoying the fresh, outdoor air. Adrian's dad was grilling steak outside, Adrian's mom was preparing a salad, and Katie was attempting to climb a 200-foot-tall tree.

"This is actually really nice," Erica said, "Outside of the nature preserve, there's not a whole lot of places where you can enjoy the outdoors."

"I agree," Adrian said. "Although, I do have to say. After a week, it does get rather dull."

"Well, it is a vacation," Erica said. "It's meant to be a break from school, work, and everything else."

Adrian nodded. "You know, Erica, there's something you need to know."

"There is?" Erica asked.

"Phoebe texted me about it this morning, and told me not to tell you, but I think you should know," Adrian said.

"Well, spill it already, then," Erica said.

"You know the two thieves who kidnapped you?" Adrian asked.

"Yes..." Erica said. "I thought the whole point of this vacation was for me to not think about them, though"

"It is," Adrian said. "But Phoebe told me this yesterday that they escaped a few days ago."

"Escaped?" Erica asked. "I'm sorry, what?"

"Phoebe told me not to tell you, since she didn't want me to ruin your vacation," Adrian said. "But I thought that it was important that you knew."

"How?" Erica asked. "How did this happen?"

"Phoebe didn't tell me," Adrian said. "Don't worry, I'm sure that the criminals won't get far. For all we know, Officer Miles or McKinley has already caught them."

"Stop trying to comfort me, okay!" Erica said. "These two men kidnapped me, beat me, and almost killed me! And now they've escaped? And you waited this long to tell me?"

"Erica, you're on vacation almost 900 miles away from North Carolina," Adrian said. "There's no way the thieves are going to hunt you down."

"It's not that," Erica said. "If the thieves have escaped, and they never get caught, it means that they'll never face justice for what they did."

"They will get caught, though," Adrian said.

"You can't make that promise, Adrian," Erica said. She pulled her phone out of her pocket and said, "I'm calling Phoebe. I need to know what's going on at home."

"Erica, it's school hours," Adrian said. "Phoebe's not going to answer."

"Then I'm calling Officer Miles," Erica said, dialing her number. I'm not going to sit here and act like everything's fine."

Adrian rubbed his forehead. "Why am I such an idiot?" he asked himself. "Why did I tell her? Phoebe was right."

"No answer," Erica said, annoyed. "She shut her phone off and headed for the RV's ladder."

"Erica, wait!" Adrian said, following her. "You-"

"Adrian, please," Erica said. "You're just making things worse. Just leave me alone for now."

Erica climbed down the ladder and went back inside the RV. She headed into her room and shut the door, locking it behind her, leaving Adrian alone of the top of the RV.

"SHOOT, I FORGOT MY phone," Miles said. "I must have left it back at the precinct."

Miles and McKinley were driving to the bank to see if they could figure out what was in the safety deposit box.

"It's fine," said McKinley, who was driving. "This shouldn't take long." He pulled the car into the parking lot of the bank and stepped outside. They stepped inside to the bank and McKinley showed the teller his badge.

"We need to see the contents of Safety Deposit Box 198," Miles said.

"Hold on," the teller said. "Let me get my manager. That's way out of my jurisdiction."

The teller left the bank window and came back shortly with a man, whom McKinley assumed to be the manager.

"Officers," the manager said. "How may I help you?"

"As I told your teller," Miles said. "We need to see the contents of Safety Deposit Box 198."

"I'm sorry Officers," the manager said. "But without a warrant, I'm afraid that I can't allow you to do that. They are *safety* deposit boxes, after all."

"This is important," McKinley said. "It's in relation to a possible murder suspect."

The manager shook his head. "I'm sure it's very important, but like I said, without a warrant, I can't show you the contents of any safety deposit box."

"Fine," Miles said, pulling a piece of paper out her bag. "Can you at least tell me if this is the same person who registered the safety deposit box?" She showed the manager a photo of Oliver Rockwood, taken from the police file.

The manager looked at the photo, then said, "Officer, this was over 10 years ago. I'm afraid that I don't memorize all our customers' faces."

Miles was getting frustrated. "What about her ID?" she asked. "I know that you scan all ID's that people provide. Can you show us the ID for the person who registered Box 198?"

The manager sighed. "Very well," he said. "But I'm only doing this to keep my name out of any scandals." He left the two officers to his office where he searched through the records of people who had registered safety deposit boxes.

"Here it is," the manager said. "The box is registered to Olive Stonewood." He pulled up the scan of Olive's ID.

Miles held the photo of Olivia Rockwood next to the ID of Olive Stonewood. "That's definitely the same person," she said. "Olivia must have registered for this safety deposit box under a false identity."

"Tell me," McKinley asked the manager. "Who pays for this safety deposit box?"

"I believe it is connected to a trust," the manager replied. "Each year, we automatically take money from the account to cover the cost of the box."

"A trust?" McKinley looked at Miles. "That must be the trust that Olivia's insurance went into. What is in that safety deposit box that's so important?"

"I don't know what either of you are talking about," the manager said. "But what I said before still stands. No warrant, no box."

"Yeah, we got that," McKinley said. "Can you print us a photo of that ID?"

The manager sighed again. "As you wish." He printed a copy of the scanned ID and handed it to Miles. "Is there anything else, officers?"

Miles and McKinley shook their heads. "Thank you very much for your cooperation," Miles said.

The two of them headed back to the car. Once they were inside, Miles said, "We need to see what's inside that box before Rockwood gets to it."

"We can't," McKinley said. "At least not without a warrant. And we don't have enough to get one."

"We need to prove that the ID Olivia used was fake," Miles said. "If we find the maker, that might give us a lead."

"Hang on," McKinley said, pulling his phone out. He dialed the precinct and Wesley picked up.

"Officer Wesley," McKinley said. "I need you to get me a list of all suspected and convicted forgers in the North Carolina area."

"You got it, Chief," Wesley said. There was a brief pause and Wesley said, "Okay, I got it. It's not a very long list, though."

"How many people are on the list?" McKinley asked.

"Just one," Wesley said. "And his name is Hubert Pickens."

"The pawn shop owner?" McKinley asked. "That idiot?"

"Yep," Wesley said. "Turns out he did a nickel for document forgery. He forged things like passports, ID's, and even checks."

"Thanks Wesley," McKinley said, hanging up the phone. To Miles he said. "I think we might want to have a chat with good 'ol Mr. Pickens."

Chapter 8

"Mr. Ryder!" Mrs. Burke's voice rang through the classroom. "What have I said about phones in my classroom?"

Scott looked up from his text conversation, and quickly put his phone away. "Sorry, Mrs. Burke," he said. "It won't happen again."

"See that it doesn't," Mrs. Burke said. "Now, since you seem so enthralled in my class, could you be so kind as to answer this question: What compound upon the addition of water produces a combustible gas?"

"Umm, Oxygen...?" Scott asked.

"Could someone who was actually paying attention answer the question, please?" Mrs. Burke asked. Remington raised her hand.

"Mrs. Cassidy?"

"Calcium Carbide," Remington said.

"Correct!" Mrs. Burke said. "At least someone was paying attention."

Scott rolled his eyes. When the class finished, Remington went over to Scott and asked, "What was that about? You've never used your phone during class before."

"Okay, the fact that you know that means that you've watched me during class before, and that's scary, but ignoring that, I got a text from Erica," Scott said. "Where's Phoebe?"

"I'm not sure," Remington said. "I've noticed that she has a different class schedule than us. Why?"

"I just need to talk to her," Scott said. "Oh, there she is!" Phoebe was walking down the hallway, digging through her backpack.

"Phoebe, wait up," Scott called. Phoebe stopped digging though her backpack and looked up.

"Scott, we have about 5 minutes in between classes," she said, continuing down the hallway. "What do you need?"

"Why would you tell Adrian about the thieves escaping?" Scott demanded.

Phoebe stopped walking. "What do you mean?"

"What do *I* mean?" Scott asked. "Adrian texted me. He told me that he told Erica what you told him, and now she's super upset."

"What? I told him not to tell her!" Phoebe said. She quickly checked her phone and saw that Erica had texted her 5 times. "Oh boy, now she's mad at me," she said, reading the texts.

"I thought that you said that we weren't going to tell her," Scott said. "That was the whole point of her going on vacation."

"I didn't tell her!" Phoebe said. "I told Adrian, because I thought he should know. We promised we'd keep them up to date on things going on back at home."

"Well, now what do we do?" Scott asked. "Are we just supposed to let this ruin Erica's vacation?"

"I don't know, okay," Phoebe said. "Look, I'll talk to her after school."

"Do not, and I mean, do not, tell her about anything that happened to us," Scott said. "That will just make her feel even worse."

"I'm not going to lie to Erica," Phoebe said. "If she asks if the thieves left town, I going to say no. Besides, don't you think she'll feel better if she knows that one of the thieves is in custody?"

"Yeah, but what about the fact that the other one almost killed Remington?" Scott asked. He checked his watch and realized that he was late for class. "We gotta go," he said. "Look, just don't say anything stupid, okay?"

"I'm just going to tell Erica the truth, alright?" Phoebe said, dashing off to class.

Scott headed off to his class as well, but he really couldn't focus on it at all. He couldn't stop wondering if not tell Erica was really the best thing to do, or if it was better that she knew.

"MR. PICKENS, I PRESUME," Miles said, walking into Pickens' pawn shop. Pickens jumped, dropping the diamond ring he was holding.

"Woah, woah, hey!" Pickens said. "What's going on? I haven't bought anymore stolen goods, I swear."

"We're not here about that," Miles said. "According to arrests records, you served time for document forgery."

"Yeah, but that was years ago," Pickens said. "I'm clean now. I got out of that business long ago."

"It was 10 years ago, to be exact," McKinley said. "However, I understand that forgers always keep copies of their forged documents. Yours were never found, so we know you must still have them."

Pickens raised his hands. "Hey man, I dunno what you're talking about," he said. "I'm just a pawn shop owner now."

"Hey, let's not forget that you purchased stolen goods," Miles said. "I let you off last time, but I don't have to do the same this time."

"Pff, dude," Pickens said. "You don't even have any proof. All the stolen stuff I had was given back to their owners. I don't even got it anymore."

McKinley tossed his phone on Pickens counter. "Congratulations. You just admitted that you had stolen goods. You should really be more careful about what you say. You never know when someone might be recording."

"Bro, what?" Pickens said. "There ain't no way that's admissible in court."

McKinley nodded. "Trust me, it is," he said. "So, how are we going to do this? I can take this recording to the District Attorney, or you can show me those fake documents that you made."

"Aw, come on man," Pickens said. "Why you gotta play dirty all the time? I'm just trying to get by."

"Pickens, this is a murder investigation," McKinley said. "Now, papers please, or this recording goes straight to the DA."

"You wouldn't do that to me, would you?" Pickens asked. "That'd just be mean."

"Don't test me," McKinley said.

"Okay, okay," Pickens said. "Dang man, you cops are so mean." Pickens went into the back room and the officers followed him.

"Hey! You can't be back here," Pickens said. "I-"

McKinley gave Pickens a stern look and he cowered. "Alright, alright," he said. Pickens walked over to a wall safe and opened it. It was filled with documents, all of which McKinley assumed were fake.

Pickens grabbed an empty box off the floor and dumped all the papers and cards into the box. "Here you go," he said. "Every document I've ever forged."

"Let's take this box back to the precinct," Miles said. "We can sort through it there."

"You're taking my stuff, man?" Pickens asked. "At least give me back my phone, bro. I spent good money on that thing."

McKinley rolled his eyes and grabbed the box of the counter. "We'll be back later." He and Miles walked over to the exit.

"Hey, what about my phone, dude?" Pickens asked. "Come on man, please!

Miles and McKinley shook their heads. "That guy," Miles said, once they were back in the car. "How does everything seem to eventually come back to him?"

"I don't know," McKinley said. "But we'd better get this box back to the precinct. It's going to take forever to sort through all of it."

"Not with the other officers' help," Miles said, pulling the car out of the lot. She drove back to the precinct and tossed the box on the table.

"Wesley, Winston!" she called. The two of them stuck theirs heads into the room. "What's up?" Winston asked.

"We need your help sorting through these documents," Miles said. "She put the photo of Oliva Rockwood on the table. We're looking for an ID for one Olive Stonewood. The photo on the ID should match the women in this photo. And the sooner we find this ID, the better."

Wesley, Winston, Miles, and McKinley all dug through the pile of documents, but they knew that it might take at least an hour before they could find the ID they were looking for.

"ERICA, ARE YOU OKAY?" Adrian asked. Erica had been in her room for the past half hour and she hadn't said anything to anyone.

"Go away Adrian," Erica called from behind the closed door. "I told you to leave me alone."

"Look, I'm sorry I took so long to tell you, okay," Adrian said. "But this is exactly why I didn't want to tell you."

Erica pulled the door open, startling Adrian. "What, so you thought it would be fine if I never knew about this?" she demanded. "You thought life should just go on like usual. 'Oh, it's fine. These two criminals might have traumatized her, but she doesn't need to know that they've escaped.' And Phoebe wasn't even going to tell me at all. That makes this even worse."

"Erica, the point of this vacation was to take your mind off of the criminals," Adrian said. "If I told you that they'd escaped, that would have completely defeated the purpose."

"Sure, take my mind off of them, since they were never supposed to be in my life again," Erica said. "Now that they've escaped, for all I know, they'll come after me again. They already came after me twice. What's preventing them from doing it a third time?"

"Nothing," Adrian said. "But you can't let them control your entire life. If you're constantly terrified of them, then you're basically just giving them what they want. They want you to be scared of them. It gives people a sense of power if other people are scared of them."

"Great, so what do I do?" Erica asked. "Pretend that everything is fine?"

"What do you do?" Adrian asked. "Enjoy your vacation. Leave everything up to Officer McKinley and Miles."

"And if they don't catch them?" Erica asked. "Then what?"

"There's still five more days left in our vacation," Adrian said. "That's five whole days for Officer McKinley and Miles to hunt them down before they have a chance to get to you."

Erica sighed. "I can try," she said. "But you don't know what it's like. The day after the police took off the ankle monitor, I couldn't stop looking around, wondering when they might come after me. It's the only reason I saw them while I was playing basketball."

"You're right," Adrian said. "I don't know what it's like. But think about the satisfaction you'll have when they're behind bars."

"I got that already," Erica said. "Then they escaped, and I'm back to being paranoid."

"Well, you'll have even more satisfaction this time," Adrian said. "Think about it this way. These two men have spent so much time and effort into tracking you down, but once they get captured, they'll realize that it was all for nothing, and the last laugh will be yours."

Erica nodded. "You're right," she said. "Officer Miles and Officer McKinley are great cops. I'm sure that they'll track the thieves down before they track me down."

"Now you're thinking the right way," Adrian said. "Just try your best to forget about them and when you come back home, everything will be resolved."

Erica nodded. "Thanks, Adrian. And I'm sorry I snapped at you. I was just so agitated and frustrated."

"It's fine," Adrian said. "Let's go get something to eat. I think Dad is done cooking."

"FOUND IT!" OFFICER Winston called out, holding an ID in his hands. He handed it to Officer McKinley, who looked closely at it.

"Name: Olive Stonewood," he read. "And the picture matches the picture of Oliva Rockwood. This is the one! Good job, Officer Winston."

"No problem, chief," Winston said.

"Now all we need to do it take this to the District Attorney and get a warrant to see the contents of that safety deposit box," Miles said. "Let's go, McKinley."

Miles peeled away from the station, and got the warrant from the DA as fast as she could. The two of them took off for the bank and Miles pulled up right in front of the bank.

The two of them entered the bank, but there was complete pandemonium going on inside. One of the tellers was clutching his arm, and the manager what trying to calm everything down.

"You," he said pointing to another teller. "Call an ambulance here. And you." He pointed to McKinley, and recognized him.

"Officers, thank goodness," the manager said. "I assume you're here in response to the robbery."

"Um, no, not exactly," Miles said. "We didn't get any calls about any robberies."

"What?" the manager demanded. "Davidson, I told you to hit the silent alarm button as soon as he left."

"I did, sir," Davidson said. "I don't know why the call didn't go through."

"I think I can answer that," one of the security guards said. "The wires connecting the alarm were snipped. This person was a professional."

"What did they steal?" McKinley asked, dreading the answer.

"Funny you should ask," the manager said. "The thief forced me to open Safety Deposit Box 198 and made off with whatever was inside."

"Which was?" Miles asked.

"Just a paper," the manager said. "That's all it was. I don't know why someone would go through all this trouble to steal a piece of paper."

"Was there something written on it?" McKinley asked.

"I don't know!" the manager said. "I was more focused on not dying, okay!"

"I got a good look at it," Davidson said. "I was standing right next to the man when he opened the box. I don't remember much of what was on it, but I remember seeing some orphanage name or something."

"An orphanage?" Miles asked. "What was the name?"

"Harmony Hovel or Haven Orphanage," Davidson said. "Something like that."

"Don't worry, he won't get very far," the manager said. "My security guard managed to shoot him in the side as he ran out. He got away in a black sedan, but he's going to need medical attention."

"Okay, I'll get Officer Wesley and Winston here to deal with the robbery," McKinley said. "We need to get to that orphanage ASAP."

Miles and McKinley dashed out of the bank and tore down the road.

"Have you ever heard of Harmony Haven Orphanage?" Miles asked. "Do you know where it is?"

"I think so," McKinley said. "It's about 10 miles from here. What I don't understand is how it's related to everything, though."

"I think I do," Miles said. "That must be what happened to Victoria Rockwood. Think about it.

Olivia Rockwood knows that her husband is trying to kill her, so she brings her daughter, Victoria to an orphanage to protect her. Since she wants to give her daughter something, she names her as the beneficiary for a $5,000,000 life insurance policy.

Steven Rockwood murders his wife, and doesn't know what she's done with their daughter. He doesn't want to take responsibility for the child, if she's ever found, though. So, he denies any knowledge of her. Then, he finds out about the life insurance policy and decides that he wants the money. So, he goes on a hunt to find out the location of the daughter."

"Okay, but what was the point of kidnapping Erica?" McKinley asked. "How does she fit into all of this?"

"Steven probably needed her to steal the documents from the safety deposit box and not himself," Miles said. "It would have been easier to send someone else in, especially if it was someone young, so the guards would be less likely to shoot them.

And I guess when he couldn't find Erica anywhere, he decided to do it himself, getting shot in the process."

"Well, let's see how true this is," McKinley said, pulling up to the orphanage. "We need to find out if Olivia Rockwood brought her daughter here."

They entered the orphanage and were greeted by the receptionist. "Officers, how can I help you?" she asked.

"We're looking for some information on a Victoria Rockwood," Miles said. "She would have been brought here about 10 or so years ago."

"One moment please." The receptionist did a search for the name, but said, "I'm sorry, no one by that name has ever been at this orphanage."

"Can you bring up a list of all the children who were entered into the system in September 2013?" Miles asked. According to the police file, Olivia Rockwood had been murdered on September 16, 2013.

"Of course," the receptionist said. She pulled up a window on her computer and showed it to the officers. "Here you go. All the children who were entered into our system in September of 2013."

The officer scanned the lists, but nothing seemed out of the ordinary. "Wait, who's this Jane Doe?" Miles asked, spotting an unnamed entry.

"Hmm, not sure," the receptionist said. "Hang on a moment." She clicked through a few pages and then said, "Ah, she was found on the front step of the orphanage on September 14, 2013. There was no information about who she was, so we took her in."

"September 14th," Miles said. "That was only about 2 days before Olivia was murdered."

"Where is this Jane Doe now?" McKinley asked.

"One second," the receptionist said, skimming through the information. "Ah, she was given the name Annabelle, and she's currently living with a foster family. Do you need their address?"

"Yes, please," Miles said. "Also, did anyone come here before us, asking for information about Annabelle?"

The receptionist shook her head. "No, but all of our records are available publicly online. I don't know exactly who has accessed them, though."

The officers looked at each other. "If the records are available online, then Rockwood might have already found out about Annabelle," McKinley said.

"Here's the address," the receptionist said, handing a piece of paper with an address written on it. "Do you mind if I ask what this is all about?"

"I'm sorry, but we have to go," Miles said. "There's no time to explain, but thank you for you help!"

"Of course," the receptionist said as Miles and McKinley rushed out to their car. Miles sped off to the address that the receptionist had given them, lights flashing, and siren blaring.

Miles pulled up to the driveway and knocked on the door. A man dressed in a ratty t-shirt and stained shorts answered the door. "Whaddya want?" he demanded. His breath smelled of alcohol and he seemed drunk.

"Who is it, Jack?" a woman's voice called out from the inside. "Tell them we're not interested."

"Whatever you're selling, we don't want any," the man said, closing the door. "Go 'way."

"Wait, sir, hang on," McKinley said, putting his foot in the door. "We're officers from the Greensboro Police Department." He pulled his badge out and showed it to the man. "We understand that you have an adoptive daughter named Annabelle?"

The man peered at McKinley. "Whozzit?" he asked. "Anna-who?"

McKinley looked at Miles, confused. "Annabelle. Are you two not foster parents to an Annabelle?"

"Who in the bloody world is Annabelle," the man demanded. He burped loudly, making Miles and McKinley both cringe. "There's no Annabelle's here. Why do people keep asking for her?"

"What do you mean by "people keep asking for her"?" Miles asked.

"A man came by about 20 minutes before you did," the woman said, joining her husband at the door. "Asked for an Annabelle. We told him we hadn't the faintest idea who she was."

"Do you two have a child at all?" McKinley asked.

"Yeah, but her name ain't no Annabelle," the man said, coughing loudly.

"Is she a foster child?" Miles asked.

"A what?" the man asked.

"She means that child that the state pays up to keep, Jack," the wife said. "So, what if we do?" she said to Miles.

"What's her name?" McKinley asked.

"What's it to you?" the woman asked. "We take care of her. She's fine."

"This is a murder investigation, okay!" McKinley said, annoyed. "Now answer my questions, or I'll have the both of you arrested."

"Wha-murder?" the man asked. "We don't got anything to do with that."

"I didn't say you did, okay," McKinley said. "Will you just answer the darn question?"

"What question?" the man asked.

"The name of the child, for goodness' sake!" Miles said. "What is the child's name and where is she?"

"What child?" the man asked.

"The foster child you take care of!" Miles said. "Did you forget the entire conversation we had three seconds ago?"

"Oh her," the man said. He turned to his wife. "What's her name again?"

"Something beginning with J," the wife said. "Julia, Jessica, Jane?"

"Seriously?" Miles asked. "You don't remember your daughter's name?"

"Oh, yeah," the man said. "I remember now. We named her Josephine!"

"Josephine, got it," McKinley said, writing the name down. "And where is she now?"

The man shrugged. "I dunno."

"Are you kidding me?" Miles said. "You are supposed to take care of her. How do you not know where she is?"

"I give her a place to live!" the man said. "That's all I gotta do. Now, leave me and my wife alone." The man slammed the door in the officers' face and Miles heard the deadbolt click.

Miles shook her head. "Does the state just allow anyone to be a foster parent?" she asked.

"Being honest, pretty much," McKinley said. "And if they can't find a better home for the child, there's not much else to do, except return them to the orphanage, and nobody wants to do that."

"That needs to be fixed," Miles said. "But right now, we need to find Josephine. Where would an 11-year-old girl be about now?"

Chapter IX

The school bell finally rang, signaling the end of the school day. Scott found Phoebe in the halls, about to call Erica.

"Phoebe wait," Scott said. "Adrian told me that everything was okay. There's no need to call Erica."

Phoebe looked suspicious. "Are you sure," she asked.

Scott nodded. "Positive. But I would really like to know where Officer Miles and McKinley are on finding the other criminal."

"Hopefully they're close," Phoebe said, packing up her backpack. "Want to walk home with me?"

"Oh-uh, I need to take Remington to my parents' store," Scott said. "She never did get to meet my parents."

"That's okay," Phoebe said. "I actually have to pick up some scallions for my mom, anyway, so I'll come with you two."

"Oh, there she is now," Scott said, spotting Remington walking down the hallway. He ran over to her and asked, "Still interested in working at my parents' store?"

Remington nodded. "Things haven't changed."

Scott laughed. "Alright, let's go." They walked out to the parking lot and Phoebe followed them, stuffing books into her backpack.

"Hey guys, wait up!" Josephine called, running up to them.

"Josephine, hi!" Remington said. "How was school?"

"Oh, it was great," Josephine said. "Remington, I wanted to ask you if you wanted to come to the library with me. I was going to spend some time drawing there."

"Sure, I'd love to," Remington said. "After I see if Scott's parents are willing to give me a job."

"Mind if I tag-along?" Josephine asked. "I don't like walking places alone."

"Of course not," Remington said. The four of them headed out of the parking lot and onto the road that Scott always took to his parents' store.

"Well, let's hope we actually make it there this time," Scott said, joking. "I- "

Before Scott could finish his sentence, a car came screaming down the road, tires smoking! All of them dove clear of the car, and the car skidded off to the side of the road. Before any of them had a chance to react, a man holding a pistol leapt from the car, and grabbed Josephine by the arm, pulling her away.

"No, hey!" Remington shouted, grabbing the man's leg and trying to pull him down. The man kicked Remington in the face, forcing her to let go and dragged Josephine to his car.

A police car with its lights flashing, and siren blaring loud enough for almost the whole town to hear screeched to a stop in front of the car. McKinley and Miles stepped out, guns drawn and pointed them at the man.

"You're done, Rockwood," McKinley said. "Let the girl go and put your hands up."

Rockwood put his finger on the trigger of his pistol. "Put your guns down, or the girl dies," he snarled. "Now!"

"You don't want to do this, Rockwood," Miles said. "It's over for you. If your finger presses that trigger, you'll be dead before you even hear the gunshot."

"I said, put your guns down!" Rockwood shouted. "I've come too far for me to fail. You've got my partner, but you're not touching me."

Miles stepped forward, slowly. Rockwood tightened his finger on the trigger. "Stay where you are!" he said. "Don't come any closer."

"I don't have a shot," McKinley said. "If I shoot him, I'll hit Josephine."

"Rockwood, listen to me," Miles said. "She's your daughter. You don't want to shoot her."

Scott, Phoebe, and Remington all looked up, not sure if they had heard correctly.

"Shut up!" Rockwood yelled, slowly dragging Josephine closer to the car. "The five million is mine. It always was. And I'll do what I have to do to get it back."

"It's not yours," Miles said. "Olivia left it to Victoria on purpose. She wanted to leave her daughter something, before you murdered her."

"You can't prove that," Rockwood said. "Nobody needs to know that I was ever here. Once I've got the five million, you'll never hear from me again."

"That's not going to happen, Rockwood," Miles said. "We will track you down. You'll never be able to hide forever."

"Tell yourself that," Rockwood said. "I-ow!"

Josephine had taken advantage of the distraction and sunk her teeth into Rockwood's arm, causing him to let Josephine go. She immediately tore loose from Rockwood's grip, giving McKinley a clear shot at Rockwood.

McKinley took the shot. It all happened in less than a second. Rockwood's eyes grew wide when he saw McKinley fire. He tried to dive out of the way, but the bullet struck him right in the chest.

Rockwood collapsed as Josephine ran to Remington and hugged her. McKinley rushed over to Rockwood, and felt his pulse. He shook his head.

"He's dead," McKinley said solemnly. "It's over."

EPILOGUE

Erica and Adrian had returned from their trip to Michigan full of stories to tell the rest of them. But first, Erica wanted to talk to McKinley to understand all the details of what had happened.

McKinley explained everything in full to Erica, who listened intently. When McKinley finished, Erica asked, "So, what exactly did they want me for?"

"Rockwood's partner told everything after he learned that Rockwood was dead," McKinley said. "Our initial hunch was correct. Rockwood wanted to have you rob the bank and steal the contents of the safety deposit box."

"Which were?" Erica asked.

"Information," Miles said. "Victoria, or Josephine's birth certificate was in there. Along with the name of the orphanage that Olivia had left Josephine at."

"I thought that she wasn't born in a hospital, though," Erica said. "How did she get a birth certificate?"

"It turns out that Victoria Rockwood traveled almost 500 miles to a hospital in Virginia to give birth," McKinley said. "That's why there was no record of her in any of the hospitals near here."

Erica whistled. "So, what does this mean for Josephine?" she asked.

"It means that Josephine finally knows who her parents are," Miles said. "And that when she turns 18, she'll have access to her mother's life insurance trust."

"Oh yeah, I almost forgot to ask," Erica said. "Before I left for vacation, about a week and a half ago, I saw a police car parked out in front of our house. I thought it was one of you, but now I'm wondering if it was one the criminals, spying on me."

"Yes, that was Rockwood," Miles said. "His partner said that after they escaped from prison, they started following you, trying to find the best time to grab you again. That's why they were so furious when you went on vacation."

Erica shuddered. She was about to ask another question, when Scott stuck his head into Miles' office. "Officer Miles?" he asked. "Can I talk to you for a second."

"Of course, Scott," Miles said. "Erica, McKinley can answer all your questions. Give me one second."

Erica nodded, and followed McKinley to his office as Scott entered Miles'.

"What's on your mind, Scott?" Miles asked.

"Remington and Josephine," Scott said. "The way they live isn't fair."

"I know, Scott," Miles said. "But unless there's someone that's willing to adopt them, there's really nothing that I can do."

"Well, what about you?" Scott suggested

"Me?" Miles asked. "You think I should adopt Remington and Josephine?"

"Think about it," Scott said. "It's perfect. You already know Remington, and she gets along so well with Josephine. They might as well already be sisters."

Miles chuckled. "Actually, Scott, it's not a bad idea. I do have extra bedrooms in my house, and you guys would be able to talk to them more. I would have to talk to McKinley about it, though."

"Officer McKinley?" Scott asked. "Why?"

Miles laughed. "Well, something you may not know, Scott, is that Officer McKinley and I are engaged."

"You are?" Scott asked.

Miles nodded. "Have been for about a month," she said. "Which would eventually make him Remington's and Josephine's adoptive father, if I do take them in."

"That is a great idea," McKinley said, walking into Miles' office. "I think adopting Remington and Josephine is almost perfect. It would be much easier for Remington to stay out of trouble with an actual parent who cares about her, and goodness knows that Josephine isn't being properly taken care of. The only question is, would they be happy with it?"

"Remington would be," Scott said. "She was talking about it with Phoebe. And Josephine spends so much time with Remington, that I think she would be happy as well."

"Well then, I just need to go down to the adoptive agency," Miles said. "CPS already knows about Remington's and Josephine's parents, and they are just itching to find them a new home. I asked them to wait until we could find someone certain, before taking them away and I think they'd be more than happy to give me custody."

"I'll tell Remington and Josephine!" Scott said. "They're in the library with Phoebe and Adrian."

"Wait for me!" Erica said, sprinting after Scott.

"WE'RE GOING TO BE SISTERS?!" Remington said, excitedly. "Did you hear that, Josephine?"

"I did, I did!" Josephine said, matching Remington's excitement. She hugged Remington again. "Sisters!"

"Wait, what about Nibbles?" Josephine asked. "Can she come along?"

Scott laughed. "Of course. I doubt that Officer Miles would object to having a guinea pig in her house."

"Yay!" Josephine said, smiling happily and practically jumping up and down. "This is the best day in the world!"

Josephine started talking to Phoebe about drawing, and showing her all the drawings, she'd made at library. Scott walked over to Remington and asked her, "So, what did my parents say? They haven't told me yet."

"They gave me the job!" Remington. "Of course, there's a lot of learning I'll have to do, but they said that I seemed like a perfect person to help them out."

"That's great!" Scott said. "Now you have a job, and since your soon-to-be adoptive mother works at the police department, I don't think you'll have to worry about people misjudging you because of your dad."

Remington nodded. "Thanks for everything you've done, Scott," she said. "And to think, this all started because I stole your wallet."

Scott laughed. "Well, I guess we're even now. You did save my life, after all."

"Hey," Phoebe said to Erica and Adrian suddenly. "We told you about everything that happened here. Now it's your turn to tell us what happened on your vacation!"

"Oh, we have stories, all right," Erica said. "Did I tell you that Adrian fell overboard while we were canoeing?"

"Hey, you weren't supposed to tell anyone that!" Adrian said, mock-offended. "And it was only because you wouldn't stop rocking the boat!"

Adrian checked his watch. "Shoot, I have to go or I'll be late for the speech team tryouts."

"Speech team?" Scott asked, curiously.

"Yeah, Erica told me that I have a way with words, so I decided to join the speech team," Adrian said. "Erica can tell you all about our vacation. I'll see you guys in a bit!"

"Wait, what about baseball?" Erica asked. "Do you still want to join the baseball team?"

Adrian shook his head. "Nope, I decided that you were right. Sports aren't my thing. I'll stick with words." He grabbed his backpack and dashed off.

Everybody turned to Erica after Adrian left. "So, are you going to tell us how the champion canoer fell overboard?" Phoebe asked.

Erica laughed. "Okay, so here's how it happened...."

THE END
A Novelette by Travis Cramer

Don't miss out!

Visit the website below and you can sign up to receive emails whenever Travis Cramer publishes a new book. There's no charge and no obligation.

https://books2read.com/r/B-A-CVTIB-RYZXD

BOOKS 2 READ

Connecting independent readers to independent writers.

About the Author

Travis Cramer is a 18-year-old storyteller with roots in the lively state of New Jersey. At 12, his family traded the hustle and bustle for the quieter charm of Delaware—a shift that left young Travis searching for adventure. With fewer distractions in his new surroundings, he turned to his love of fiction as an outlet for creativity. What started as a simple hobby soon transformed into a mission: to write a full-fledged story, beginning to end. From this spark of inspiration, *Misadventure and Mystery* was born—a series where imagination knows no bounds, and every page brims with excitement and intrigue.

Read more at https://books2read.com/ap/81Do3O/ Travis-Cramer.